RECIPE FOR A CURSE

LISSA KASEY

D1518700

Recipe for a Curse

1st Edition

Copyright © 2020 Lissa Kasey

Cover Art by Doelle Designs

Edited by Indie Pride, LLC

Published by Lissa Kasey

http://www.lissakasey.com

With the excitement of the holidays over, the cold settling in on a planned month of quiet seemed to deepen the usual January chill. My grocery lists were much shorter, meal planning only taking a few hours a day, and prep was fast and easy. The manor was on winter break, as my boss Zach Frank, called it. No classes, no guests, just a few weeks of quiet after the stress of the holidays.

I had to admit that a break was nice. The handful of small holiday parties and last minute craft classes that turned into a gift exchange, had been sort of crazy. My days had become endless, dawn to dusk, cooking, planning, and even serving when the parties got too busy. The one thing I still took time for each week was taking food to the local food bank.

Once a week, the two local groceries closest to the house loaded up my little Matrix and sent me to the food bank. It was always canned goods and processed foods, but necessary. Often, I brought bread baskets of freshly made loaves, and these past few weeks, a mix of cookies and pies. The handful of families needing the food often waited for me on Wednesdays to get first dibs. A few of the other volunteers drove stuff out to those without transportation and the elderly who didn't drive. People didn't like to think their quiet towns or pockets of wealth housed those with food insecurity, but I'd found that it was a reality everywhere. Even in upstate New York, buried in a small tourist area with large plots of land. I always made sure there was enough for everyone. Those with nothing, and those with only a little.

Today one face had been absent. In fact, I hadn't seen him in a few weeks. Rio wasn't always at the food bank. I knew he lived in a trailer on a tiny piece of land that didn't even have a road leading to it. He had a car, but it didn't always work. In the nicer months he'd hike down and catch a ride. But with the heavy snow, and brutal wave of cold that had dropped over the weekend, maybe he hadn't been able to come down. That worried me.

"Has anyone seen Rio?" I asked Diana as she helped unload the last of the boxes of canned goods from my car. The small crowd had already chosen their pies and cookies from my stash.

"Hey, Montana," Jim called as he reached for the stack Diana brought to him. "Everyone has been gushing about how amazing your pies were for the holidays. How grateful they were to have them."

I felt heat rise into my face. The compliments shouldn't have embarrassed me. I was a trained chef. Pastries were a hobby to my cooking passion, and the holidays gave me opportunities to share my skills. The manor had even been open to the locals for a holiday dinner I'd prepared. That way everyone had a chance to have turkey, ham, and all the trimmings. We had to schedule times so we hadn't been overcrowded, but the day had gone smoothly and the joy filled faces had made my holiday.

Sean, Zach's fiancé, had helped create small gift baskets for everyone local filled with baked goods, small crafts like handkerchiefs, safety masks designed to be almost medical grade while still fun and cute, and wooden puzzle toys. I'd never met anyone more skilled at making things than Sean. He'd even helped me perfect a few recipes of some Chinese pastries and steamed buns that had become a favorite at the manor. I'd brought a couple dozen to the food bank this week and had been hoping to push a dozen or so off on Rio so I knew he was eating more than beans and ramen.

"Thank you," I told Jim. "Have you seen Rio?"

"Not since Christmas at the manor," Jim said.

Diana shook her head. "He hasn't been in at all. I've been a bit worried. After we had that big drop in temperature, and he's out so far... I know his car hasn't been working for a while."

I gnawed at my lip a bit in worry as I helped them stock the shelves. "I could drive up; it's not that far past the manor, right?" I tried to recall the gravel trail that veered into the woods, but I had only ever driven past it. Would it be lost in the snow? He was only a mile or so from the main road; though far enough that he had no actual address. I wasn't even sure he had power, and now that I thought about it, that worried me too. We'd hit single digits in the last week, dropping overnight below zero.

"It's a bit of a hike from the road. You won't be able to drive close at all," Jim said. "Trees are too thick even when there isn't snow. He's probably hunkered down for the winter like he usually is."

I tried to think back to last year, but I'd been new to the area, and hadn't started the food bank runs yet. With the manor on holiday, and my new kitchen already stocked full, it wasn't like I had a lot to do. I had a cooler full of food for the manor in the car, but it was just stuff I'd gotten on sale or in bulk to refill basics like flour, sugar, salt, a few pounds of steak, and a giant bag of rice. Taking the time to check on Rio wouldn't set me back at all, and if it would stop the anxiety welling up in my stomach, that would be a bonus.

Of course, the thought that he might have gotten sick crossed my mind. Our small town has been very strict about mask guidelines, especially after a visitor showed up just before Thanksgiving bringing the virus with them. After a half dozen were infected, with the entire town up in arms and contract tracing, we'd shut it down fast. But maybe Rio hadn't been so lucky. Maybe he had visitors over the holidays we didn't know about. Which of course made me think back to our holiday party and how many people might have been exposed. The tables had been ten feet apart, windows open for ventilation, and masks required while people weren't eating. Everything disinfected and sanitized to death. Zach worked hard to follow health guidelines to ensure the staff was safe even while feeding the community. The gift baskets we'd given out had provided at least a week's worth of food. And since the staff had all been tested before and after the event, I hoped no one had it.

Though since it had been several weeks since Christmas, I thought it unlikely someone wouldn't have displayed symptoms. Maybe Rio had been the unlucky one. That thought worried me even more.

"He doesn't come down much in the winter," Diana agreed. "It's why we always let him take a little extra. He stocks up for the worst few months of the year. Poor guy still comes down in the spring looking like a skeleton."

Rio hadn't looked like a skeleton when he'd come to the holiday feast. He looked good. Wide through the shoulder, hair a bit long and wild, but clean and bright eyed. He looked of Greek or Italian ancestry but I didn't know for sure. He had mentioned once to Zach that he'd been in the military, and used some sort of disability pay as his income. He'd grown up in New York City, that much I knew. I had tried not to be nosy, but couldn't help watching him. He was pretty in a rugged way, like Zach was in a bear sort of way.

I'd probably made a fool of myself flirting. Being small, pretty, and the definition of a twink, I'd sort of naturally fallen into the fem boy habits I'd picked up working in the big city. Being flirty and cute used to bring in the guys like bees to honey. Didn't work so well out here in the middle of nowhere. And I had to admit I was lonely.

Rio always smiled and nodded, at least appearing to listen. We'd never had long conversations, especially now that the virus scared most of us away from social situations. But I did try to make him feel like he wasn't so alone.

Watching Zach and Sean over the holidays, seeing them glow with happiness, hold hands, or sit cuddled together near one of the massive fireplaces, had made me want that for myself. Maybe I'd make a trip into the city soon. Take a few days and see if I could meet some people. Though swiping left felt really hollow right now, when what I really wanted was someone to smile at me the way Zach smiled at Sean. Like I was their world.

I still didn't feel safe randomly hooking up with someone. Too much illness around. And didn't that put a damper on my love life. The world at large taught us that sex was crucial. In truth it wasn't sex so much as human interaction. The last year of stunted contact had really hammered that point home.

Rio had a nice smile. Warm and kind, though guarded, he'd always seemed very genuine. And now I was really worried. "Skeleton?" But I'd spent some time living off ramen myself before Ms. Sofia had found me. Not balanced meals by any means. "Does he even have power up there?"

"I think he has a generator," Jim shrugged. "He doesn't like people much. Keeps to himself. Heard someone say he has a bit of PTSD. But he's been up here ten years or so? No one sees him in the winter. Then spring he shows up."

"And no one worries about him all winter?"

"Most of us are too busy to get up that way," Diana admitted. The manor was almost thirty minutes north, and with Rio's tiny plot of land being past that, it made sense. In the snow it would be even harder. The roads were always well plowed, but since he wasn't on a dedicated road, it was unlikely he'd be anything more than snowed in most of the winter. Crap.

"I'll stop up," I said making a commitment right that minute that I would not let that man spend months in the miserable cold all alone. "Can I load up a box for him?" What were some of the things he normally picked?

"Sure," Jim said. "Take whatever you need."

I went through the pantry, choosing things that could stretch meals, canned chicken, green beans, stuffing, and even got a few fresh items including a sack of potatoes and some bananas. I loaded it all into paper bags, got directions from Jim and headed back up, dialing Zach from the car on the way.

"I wanted to let you know where I'm going," I told my boss. "In case I'm not back till late or something. It sounds like it's a bit of a walk."

"There's a storm coming," Zach said, sounding worried. "Ten inches of snow predicted. This far north you know it's more likely we'll get over a foot."

"I've got my coat and stuff," I said. "It's not far. Just seven or so miles from the manor."

"Call if there's trouble. I've put the plow on my truck and can tow a car out of a ditch if necessary."

"I will," I promised and hung up. My plan was to send him the coordinates as soon as I arrived. I accidentally drove by the outlet twice before finding a small break in the snow. It almost looked like someone had partially shoveled the edge of the road where the trail began. I pulled off, parking out of the way, and sent a text off to Zach. I only had one bar on my phone, so hopefully it went through. Jim hadn't been kidding about the trail. It was literally nothing more than a thin hiking trail etching through the trees. I couldn't see anything but a dark overlay of woods.

When I opened the back of the car I cursed, realizing that I had no real way to carry pounds of food to a cabin that was a mile or so away through the snow. I stared at the cooler. It was a giant thing with wheels and a handle. That would have to do. I pulled out the cooler, which only had five pounds of bacon and a pack of steaks in it, loaded it with as much as I could, then stacked what I was able to on top before locking up the car. There was more he could have, but I'd have to make another trip back.

I tugged on the thick winter coat I almost never wore, a hat, and some gloves, then pulled the cooler to the trail. The wheels were almost useless. The snow on the path was shoveled, but not sturdy enough to roll on, so it was like pulling a lead weight. It wasn't until I hit a dozen or so yards into the trees that the cooler seemed to find ice and begin to slide.

Thank god.

There were tracks along the edge of the trail. I examined them as I walked. Rabbit I thought, since they were small and sort of looked like a dick dragging through the snow. It made me laugh a little. A wild dick running through the woods, a meme I'd seen a few times but could actually fit it to factual life. City boy like me wouldn't normally know much about wildlife, but Zach had arranged for a local hunter to come in and give mini tours of the woods, and how to identify critters. I admit I took it because the forest surrounding the manor was endless and very intimidating. I'd had lots of nightmares since starting the job about being snatched by mountain lions or bears. The hunter assured us that both were rare even in the manor's huge stretch of woods. He'd given us a little e-guide of footprints to keep saved on our phone. Birds, squirrels, and rabbits were easy. The bigger stuff we were to avoid if we saw a hint of a handful of things. The class had helped ease some worries, but I kept my eyes peeled.

After several yards there were a scattering of bigger tracks. Okay well, they were huge. I paused to look at them, holding my hand beside one to make sure I was seeing what I was seeing. Yeah, bigger than my hand. Wolf, maybe? Nature queen I was not. But it looked sort of like a dog print. Big ass dog, or wolf. Should I go back?

I looked around, wary of the woods now, though the tracks

disappeared into the trees heading away from the trail. No sign of movement. Hopefully that wolf was napping somewhere far away after its little rabbit chase.

Turning back to the supplies, I tugged it and we rolled along for a while, me just following the trail and hoping it would lead me somewhere. The cold was more intense out here. Wind not as strong as the trees acted as a good break, but the temperature almost seemed to drop. I tugged my jacket up and hat down, leaving little more than my eyes clear. Could eyes freeze? They sort of felt like it.

CHAPTER 2

As snow began to fall, I wondered if this had been the dumbest idea on the planet. It would have been smarter to go back to the manor and have Zach deliver the supplies. He had a truck and could probably think of a thousand ways to make this easier and safer. What if Rio didn't even need anything? It had only been three weeks since the Christmas dinner. He was probably fine. Hunkered down to keep warm.

I'd have really liked to be warm in that moment, could even think of my favorite mulled cider recipe. Did I have all the ingredients for it back home? Probably. I kept the kitchen well stocked. The short time I'd lived in youth shelters and been food insecure had really taught me to prepare. Even if the power went out at the manor, I'd have enough food to feed everyone for a few weeks at least, although I might have to get a little creative.

Apocalypse ready, no, but regular snowstorms I could handle. Thankfully the manor hadn't had any incidences since Zach and Sean had become a thing. Guess true love had broken that curse.

I sighed thinking of their relationship and craving it hard for myself. I wouldn't have to wait until I was in my forties, right? That would suck. Did anyone want to wait twenty years for love?

The trail went on. At least someone had shoveled it. It would be nice to know that I was walking somewhere instead of following a path to the middle of nowhere, which is what it felt like in that moment. The snow began to accumulate, and my feet felt numb. Tennis shoes weren't really meant for snow adventures I thought, and wondered if I should have splurged on that pair of designer boots I'd seen online. The fur insides would probably have been a dream right now. But they hadn't been practical since my trips outside the manor were short and limited to plowed parking lots and my car.

How long had I been walking anyway? It felt like forever.

My breath made the material around my face moist, and a chill settled into my bones like I couldn't recall having ever felt. But I kept pulling, walking along that tiny path hoping to find something. A hut, maybe? A sauna would have been really great right that minute, or even just a fire. I might drop myself in it right that second for the moment of blazing warmth before I died.

"Dramatic much, Montana?" I lectured myself. "Seriously, you've been walking for less than a half an hour. Phone says it's twenty degrees. That's balmy compared to the negative temps we had over the weekend. Suck it up, buttercup."

Jim said it was a little more than a mile. Hadn't I walked that far already? I huffed out a tired breath and kept walking. Stupid snow, falling around me, blanketing my feet until my movement was little more than a shuffle to keep the cooler moving. My arms would ache tomorrow. Gym bunny I was not. Running around the kitchen had always been my choice of exercise.

Then the cooler stopped completely, jammed into the snow and a mix of half frozen ice.

"Fuck," I cursed the stupid thing, turning to tug. The weight must have been too much because the handle popped off instead, sending me flying backwards, slipping on ice, arms flailing for a moment as I tried to keep my balance, and then falling, landing in a pile of snow. At least it was fresh snow so the only real pain came from having my feet slide out from under me, twisting one of my ankles in a way that it throbbed as I lay there.

The snow landed on me in little magical flakes of pretty lace. Beautiful, but quickly melting as they latched onto my eyelashes. I stared at them while they peppered my face with cold, contemplating the effort of getting up. Maybe calling for help. Though I was pretty sure my phone wasn't going to work this far into the middle of nowhere.

Then a face loomed over me and I screamed. Couldn't help that it was a high-pitched shriek of terror as I hadn't heard anything but the wind and snow. And who expected anyone to appear over them like some sasquatch in the falling snow?

The face pulled back as I sat up, and I slapped a hand over my mouth. Facts taking a few seconds longer to register before I could stop screaming and suck in air. "Rio! I'm so fucking glad to see you. You scared the crap out of me. Sorry!"

Rio crouched a few feet away, no jacket, just jeans tucked into boots, with a thick sweater over the top. His hair hanging to his shoulders in thick dark waves, and his face scruffy with beard overgrowth. His eyes, that crystal clear pale blue I'd found eerily alluring, gazed at me with worry. He looked like he could have walked off the cover of an old-fashioned romance novel. Okay he was scruffier than that, and that was just fine. I liked my men a bit hairier than most.

"You shouldn't be out here," he said, his tone deep, but without accent. "Are you okay?"

When I didn't move immediately, he came closer and offered a hand. "Montana?"

"Sorry, sorry. I'm fine, I promise." I told him and took his hand and tried to get up. The second I put pressure on my ankle it screamed in pain and I had to take my weight off it, sending me sliding backward and pulling Rio with me.

He caught himself, landing only half on top of me and in the snow with an "Oof!" of surprise.

"Sorry! Crap," I grumbled. "Must have twisted my ankle when I slipped." His weight felt good on me, but he scrambled away and back to his feet, dusting off the snow. I dug out my phone, hoping to call Zach for a rescue. "No service. Crap."

"What are you even doing out here in the middle of a blizzard?" Rio asked. He knelt carefully beside my feet and examined them. The right ankle screamed at the slightest touch. I couldn't hide my flinch, or the heat that filled my face.

"Bringing you supplies. I thought I could make it before the storm hit." But the snow around us was no longer tiny flakes, it was giant clumps of white. Even the trail was being swallowed by the piles of accumulating cold. Would I be able to find my way back to my car? "They said at the food bank that you don't come down much in the winter, and I hadn't seen you since Christmas, so I was worried…" I began to ramble, feeling stupid. "Packed as much as I could for you in the car, but didn't realize it was so far, so there's more. It's in the car… but I have a lot in the cooler and the bags on top."

Rio sighed and leaned down to scoop me up. Having never been picked up like a damsel in distress in my life, but always having dreamt of it, I had to say it was both a dream come true, and a total embarrassment. His warmth, the strength and ease in which he seemed to lift me and then hold me close, was great. But I felt like an idiot for getting myself into trouble. He glanced at the cooler and the stack on top.

"I'll come back for it. You feel like a giant ice cube," he remarked. He was deliciously warm. Thankfully he didn't look sick either, which had been a big worry.

He turned and headed into the trees. I hoped his place wasn't far. But what we came upon wasn't really what I'd expected. It was a trailer, the old-school seventies kind with rusted yellow walls and a tin roof. The entire base of it was stacked with firewood and if it had seen better days, they'd been decades before. There was a chimney with smoke dancing around it. I hoped it was warm at least.

He opened the door and carried me inside, but the chill lingered. We got to the living room area, a narrow space with a large fireplace and nothing else other than a nest of blankets, and he set me down. He pulled the blankets up around me, then vanished outside for a minute only to return with more wood, adding it to the fire, and stoking it to a blaze. Why hadn't he had that up higher before? The inside of the house was downright chilly. I could see doors in the distance closed, and the tiny kitchen looked clean but empty. Other than the nest of blankets, it was almost like no one lived here.

"I'll be right back," Rio said and headed out the door.

The heat from the fire began to warm me and the living room. At least it worked. When Rio returned it was with the cooler and bags of supplies. He set them inside the door, then came in and shut the two layers of doors before kicking off his shoes.

"You won't get a signal on your phone until the storm passes. Even then they don't always work. Does anyone know you're here?" Rio asked. He padded my way in bare feet and I wondered how he wasn't half frozen to death.

"My boss."

"Mr. Frank? He'll come looking as soon as the storm passes."

He probably would. "Yes," I agreed.

Rio headed down the hall, opened a door that appeared to be to a bathroom, and then returned with a first aid kit. "Let me look at that ankle of yours." He eased my shoe off and pushed the bottom of my jeans up, the material soaking wet and cold. Even my sock was sopping. When had that happened?

He stripped off the sock. "It's best to keep your feet dry in this sort of cold. Anything else is asking for frostbite."

"You're not even wearing socks," I pointed out. "How are you not frozen?"

"I run warm," he said, his hands gently running over my foot and ankle. "No broken bones, but you might have torn a ligament. Those are a bitch to heal. I can wrap it, immobilize it. You'll probably have to stay off it for a while." He began pulling things out of the first aid kit.

"You know a lot about medicine?"

"Was a combat medic for a couple tours. Worked as an EMT before that."

That surprised me. Why wasn't he doing that anymore?

"I don't handle blood well," he said without me having to ask, "or stress, anymore."

"Oh," I said. That would make doing medical stuff hard.

"You should get these wet clothes off," he said after wrapping my ankle up. The bandages were tight enough they hurt, but also felt like they were keeping everything in place. "Let me find you some things to keep you warm." He looked at me, and down at my pants which were soaked. Pink stained his cheeks. "You should probably take those off too. Better safe than sorry."

He scrambled up and away, back down the hall to another closed door and inside. Was I reading him right? Was he into me? Straight men didn't normally blush at other men being half nude around them. My heart gave a little flip-flop. Silly, to be injured and sitting in a trailer that didn't appear to have working electricity, and thinking that the guy was hot for me. Maybe I was desperate, but I did like Rio. The handful of conversations we had didn't make me think he hated people, just that he was sort of quiet, and that was okay.

I began pulling off the gloves and jacket. The bottom of my sweater was wet, my pants all the way up my thighs, and despite the heat, the icy chill against my skin was growing. I wriggled out of my shirt, even unbuttoned my pants, hoping to push them off and wrap myself in a blanket before he returned. But the fact that they were skinny jeans and wet, meant they were not coming off without a fight, and my ankle hurt from too much movement.

Fuck. I got the pants to my thighs, wishing I'd picked undies that weren't covered in rainbow hearts that day, but not sure what else to do. I wrapped a blanket around me as Rio returned with a ball of clothes in his hands. It was a hoodie.

"This should be big enough for you to swim in," he said holding it out to me. "It will help warm you up."

I carefully took it, trying to keep the blanket around me and not flash him my undies, even while weirdly immobilized by my wet jeans. "Can't get my jeans off, they are stuck from the wet and my ankle hurting."

He raised a brow but knelt down and tugged carefully, pulling the fabric off my good leg first, then carefully over my wrapped ankle, which had apparently swollen to three times its size. There was no avoiding that pain, but I bit my lip hard not to cry out. But finally, free of the wet fabric, the warmth of the fire began to ease into my bones.

"Thank you," I told him and tried to pull on the hoodie while keeping the blanket around me. He turned away to give me a bit of privacy, dragging everything to the kitchen area and unpacking.

"Do you have a dog?" I asked, finding some hair on the blanket that didn't seem to be his. I'd never had a pet myself, but enough of my culinary school friends had. It wasn't people hair that clumped up like that.

"Not really," he answered, which I thought was odd. "Are you allergic?"

"No. At least I don't think so. Never had a dog." Had always thought of myself as more of a cat person. Dogs, while always happy to see their owner, sort of read as high maintenance to me, and I was high enough maintenance just for me.

"This is a lot of food," he said.

"I picked things that I thought would last well. Easy to work with. I can think of a dozen recipes to make with this stuff." I struggled into the hoodie. He'd been right about swimming in it.

It was a two extra large and since I wore a medium on the best of days, it was long, fluffy and when I tugged it over my butt, I could have worn it as a dress. I tucked my good leg into it and left my bad one stretched out and covered it with the blanket. "I was really worried you were sick too, so I brought stuff for soup."

"I never get sick. And I'm not much of a cook," Rio said. He organized cans into a couple small cupboards, most of which were pretty bare, then opened the cooler. His eyes widened. "There is steak and bacon in here. Did you mean to bring that?"

"Yes. Got them at the butcher for a deal. There's plenty at the manor. Thought maybe you could use them."

Heat turned Rio's face pink again and he looked away. "I'll have to store them in the cooler outside. Fridge doesn't work."

"Does the stove work? I could make us some food."

Rio turned away. "Everything's electric. Powers been off for a while. Can't afford the bill."

"Jim mentioned a generator?"

"Generators take gas. That's not free either, plus getting it filled when I don't have a car is damn near impossible." He let out a long sigh. "All I have is the fire. I should wrap you up and take you back to your car. Maybe the roads are clear still." Though when we both glanced toward the window, and the heavy rush of falling snow, I knew there wasn't a chance of that. The plows would do the main part of town first, which was a half an hour south. They'd get out here eventually, but it would likely mean my car would be plowed into the tiny alcove I'd pulled into.

"Do you have camping stuff? Like a cook pot? I can make stuff over the fire." Another class at the manor I'd taken. Honestly, I'd have taken everything if I'd had time. The survival stuff had appealed to me because we were out so far and the manor used to lose power from time to time. Zach had created solar charging stations and backup generators so it didn't happen anymore, but he was prepared that way. "I can make us some stew."

"Bacon and steak stew?" Rio sounded dumbfounded and obviously hungry.

I smiled. "Some potatoes and carrots too, if you don't mind. They are in the bags if they aren't completely frozen. If they are, well I'll have to cut them either way. I could use some food too."

Rio stared at me for a minute, like he wasn't sure I was saying what he thought I was, but finally he began to dig through the kitchen pulling out some basic camping supplies, a cutting board, and even giving me a good hunting knife. He piled up stuff around me. "What do you need from the supplies you brought?"

I listed off some of the things I knew were in the bags with a plan to create a hearty, protein packed meal that would last a few days. "And water," I finished.

Rio paused in gathering to glance not at the sink, but outside. He looked down. "I'll have to melt some snow."

I processed that for a minute. "As long as it's not yellow, sure," I joked.

Rio didn't seem to catch the joke. "There's a well, but it's frozen…"

"Rio, it's fine. We only need about two cups anyway. I'm sure we can get that in this snowstorm in a minute."

He nodded, but wouldn't look at me. Instead, he brought over the piles of food, then vanished outside with a small bowl. He had a good-sized Dutch oven with feet, and heat resistant gloves, so I opened the grate separating the fire from the room and carefully set the pot close, leaving off the lid so I could fill it. He was gone a few minutes while I cut up things and added the bacon to the pot first. Once it began to sizzle, I knew we'd get enough heat to have ourselves a fine meal. Too bad I didn't have a way to make a loaf of crusty bread to go with it.

CHAPTER 3

Whether he returned, he paused just inside the doorway and sniffed, breathing deep.

"Bacon," I smiled at him. "Almost as divine as fresh bread. I'm assuming you're not vegan?"

"No," he said, "not vegan at all. I eat a lot of rabbit in the winter. Sometimes deer."

It made sense that he'd hunt for food, though I didn't see a gun anywhere. Maybe it was in one of the locked rooms. Odd how normally guns made me nervous, but I didn't feel at all uneasy about being in his space. "How do you hunt when you don't like blood?"

"Rabbits don't have much. Deer... sometimes when I'm hungry, it doesn't matter." He brought over the bowl and it was filled with snow, fresh and clean looking.

"Thank you. Sit, get warm. It's freezing out there. It will just take a few minutes to get the meat going and then I can add everything else."

"How long does it take to cook?" Rio perched on the other side of the fireplace.

"Depends on the fire. Once everything is in the pot, it will have to come to a boil and cook for a half an hour or so. As long as I cut the veggies small, they will cook fast. Hungry?"

He looked away again, but licked his lips. I really hoped he wasn't out of food already, but the small glimpse I'd seen of his cupboards, there hadn't been much. "Yes," he admitted. He glanced toward the window. "Think your boss will be here before dark? You said you told him where you'd be?"

I nodded. "I did tell him. He might look for me before then. Dinner for the manor is already done. Ana would finish it if I'm not there to pop it in the oven. So, maybe not? Depends on if he's distracted by Sean. Zach doesn't always come to the manor for dinner and right now everyone is on winter break. He doesn't really have a reason to."

"Sean?"

"Zach's lover? Partner? I think you met him at the holiday dinner. Pretty Asian man?"

"There were lots of pretty Asian men at the manor..." Rio remarked.

There had been. And that he noticed, made me hopeful, even if I wasn't one of those pretty Asian men. "Long white hair. Usually in a braid."

Rio thought for a moment, then nodded. "He was unusual."

That was an odd comment as I didn't find Sean all that unusual. Pretty. Insanely talented when it came to crafts and anything handmade. Resourceful, as he could recreate any recipe I showed him, even if it meant changing half the ingredients around because we were out of things. But unusual? Huh.

"How so?" I inquired.

"Just seems different..." Rio said.

I wondered briefly if it was because Sean was Asian? I'd never sensed that from Rio before, but racism hid in a lot of small ways I'd only recently begun to notice. "He's amazing. Smart, sweet, and madly in love with Zach."

"People in town don't mind that?" Rio said after a few minutes of watching me work. I added the water and vegetables before putting the lid on to let the soup cook.

"Mind what? That Zach is gay or that he has an Asian lover?"

Rio seemed to think on that for a few minutes. "Both, maybe? Gay mostly. Lots of Asian people in town. Though I guess the world has been sort of crazy this year."

"I've never noticed anyone in town say anything. Zach is sort of a big guy, so…" The handful of the hateful, as I called them, had been pretty silent since early fall when the businesses on the small Main street had gotten together and been very forceful with their rules. Safety had been key. That meant anyone giving one business crap was banned from all of them. So gay, Asian, or even vegan, it didn't matter. I'd been afraid to go to the grocery store for a few weeks. When I'd mentioned it to my boss, he'd accompanied me and had a long conversation with the owners that had put the entire business community of our small town on the same page.

The manor brought tourism, money, jobs, and renewed interest in our cold, sleepy area even during the winter. Only a handful of months and the dying town had become a thriving community. No one wanted on Zach's bad side. "I feel pretty safe wherever I go," I added.

"Even here in the middle of nowhere?" Rio grumbled. "There could be monsters out here."

Weird choice of words. "Like bears and mountain lions?" I asked, not really thinking of them as monsters, but I knew that some people did.

He shrugged.

"Animals hunt to eat. As long as I stay out of their way, I'm fine. I'd be more worried about getting lost in the woods than some critter getting me." I held out my arms. "I'm sort of stringy, can't imagine there's enough meat on me to satisfy the smallest predator."

Rio's gaze roamed over me, like he was really assessing

whether or not I'd taste good, and oddly it felt more than just physically hungry. The edges of predatory, really. I don't know why his attention suddenly made me warm, but the tiny trickles of danger made my heart beat a little faster, and my cock harden. The idea of Rio's mouth on me turned me on. Okay, so maybe I was a little masochistic and hadn't known it.

I licked my lips, swallowing hard and Rio's gaze came up, eyes softening as he seemed to look at my mouth and then meet my eyes. He gave me a soft smile and looked away shyly. Like he'd been thinking of tasting me in other ways. I let out a long breath, trying to rein in the attraction. The guy was obviously hungry. No need to get all hot and bothered while his tummy was growling.

"There is pumpkin bread in the foil wrap," I pointed toward the last unpacked bag on the counter. "If you're hungry and want to nibble. There's also a jar of honey somewhere."

Rio glanced toward the kitchen, swallowing visibly as he stared at the bag, like he wanted to leap toward it and eat everything. But he didn't move.

"It's okay," I said. "Get the bread. I'd love a slice too, if you don't mind."

Only then did he move, almost deliberately slow, getting off the hearth of the fireplace and heading to the kitchen. He unpacked the last bag, full of canned chicken, tuna, and even beef, then finding the container full of mincemeat mini pies and finally the bread and honey.

I pretended to poke at the stew while he tried to stealthily eat a couple of mini pies. How long had he been without food? I was determined now to fill his pantry this winter, even if it meant daily trips into the woods. When he finally returned with the bread and honey, I retrieved the cutting board to slice thick chunks and slather them with honey.

"Eat," I commanded him, handing over four giant slabs of bread and honey. "My pumpkin bread is divine."

He devoured them, licking the honey off his fingers as he went. I pretended not to watch, but couldn't help being thrilled he liked it. Either that or he was so hungry he'd eat anything. Odd how he did look a bit thinner than he had over the holidays. It had only been a few weeks.

Once the stew was up to a boil and smelling heavenly, I poked at the potatoes to make sure they were tender. "Looks like the stew is ready. Do you have some bowls?"

Rio headed to the kitchen again, returning with some thick stoneware bowls and a couple of big spoons. I filled his bowl to the top and handed it over, before adding a much smaller amount to mine. The stew tasted a bit like a bacon burger. Too bad I hadn't thought to bring cheese.

I licked the spoon. "Yum. Haven't had this in ages."

Rio paused to stare at me, eyes a bit big.

"You okay?" I asked.

He nodded and ducked his head to shovel more food in his mouth. But he paused again as though watching me eat made him feel weird.

"Eat," I told him. "As much as you want. I love seeing people enjoy the food I make. It's why I'm a chef. I remember the first time I made a batch of cookies and gave them to some school friends. It wasn't anything special, but they loved them, and I remember feeling like I could fly."

"You're a good cook. The soup is good, and the bread too." Rio looked at the bread, which he'd eaten most of, and then the stewpot.

I waved at the pot. "Eat. I'm good, I promise."

He refilled his bowl twice more while I slowly made my way through mine. Warmth finally broke through and began to make me sleepy. I set my bowl down and snuggled deeper into the pile of blankets. Was Rio cold? He was barefoot again, his hair slightly damp from the trips outside. I watched him pick up our bowls and move them to the kitchen. He organized the supplies and ate another three pies before putting the leftovers away.

I must have nodded off because movement of the stewpot startled me awake. I blinked at him as he used the gloves to carry the pot to the kitchen. The grate was back in place in front of the fire, and I was blessedly warm.

"Sorry," I said. "I don't know why I'm so tired."

"Battling the cold will do that," Rio said. "The snow is still coming down hard." He sounded worried. "I hope your boss comes soon."

"Am I taking up all your blankets?" I struggled to free myself from the nest. "I'm okay by the fire."

"It's fine," Rio said. "I told you I run warm. I'm okay."

"At least come sit by the fire. I won't bite, I promise."

He flinched. Had I said something wrong? Maybe I'd read him wrong and he was afraid of being close to another man?

"Rio?"

He let out a long puff of air and made his way over, carefully lowering himself down onto the blankets. "How's your ankle?"

"Throbbing," I admitted. "Still think it's a ligament?"

His head bobbed. "Yeah, bones are more of an ache than a throb when broken. You'll probably have to get it immobilized. They don't usually do casts for that, but a walking brace maybe, and instructions to keep off of it."

That was going to suck. How would I move around the kitchen and still keep it immobile?

The wind howled, whipping hard enough that the walls shook. A waft of frigid air seemed to pour into the space and I shivered. Would the walls even hold? Rio moved closer, digging into the blanket nest himself, and leaving us practically on top of the fireplace.

"Haven't really had money for repairs," Rio admitted. "Even if there was much of a way to fix it. Was nice back when I first bought it. Walls and a roof. That was all I thought I needed. Well, that and space." He curled up close, using the wall as a back brace, even though I thought being that close to the wall was like sitting on an ice cube.

"Did it help? Having the space?" I asked, wondering if the comments about his PTSD were true, and if being out here, away from everyone, really helped.

"At first?" He tucked the blankets until they were around us and I sat close enough to him to feel his heat too. He did run warm. A bit like having a personal heater. "I thought being away from everyone was good."

"It sounds lonely."

"Sometimes," he agreed. He reached over and lifted me like I weighed nothing, shifting the blankets around so we both had a big pile. "I hope your boss comes before dark."

"What happens after dark?"

He was silent for a few minutes before saying, "The cold gets worse."

"We can keep the fire going. You have lots of firewood."

"Never lasts. No matter how much I cut, it's never enough…"

Did that mean he went part of the winter without heat? How was that possible? I frowned at him, but he stared into the flames instead. I closed my eyes and let the heat soothe all my worries. Even if it was only for a few minutes, it was okay. I didn't think Rio would hurt me, or let anything hurt me. And the storm raising a fuss outside made me want to nap. Since I couldn't tell from the light coming through the windows what time it was, I figured it didn't much matter if it was two in the afternoon or seven at night. A nap sounded great.

CHAPTER 4

A pounding on the door barely roused me, but the movement around me had me blinking into the dark of the room. The fire had faded to little more than a few embers, and I could feel the chill where the blankets didn't cover my face. But Rio was up and moving as though we'd been caught doing something much more intimate than sharing a blanket.

The pounding came again. "Hello?" I heard a familiar voice call.

"It's Zach," I told Rio, and scooted upright, wincing when my ankle screamed at me. "Stupid ankle."

Rio opened the door, and I was surprised to see the snow piled up midway in the frame, but Zach stood below the steps, bundled up like an Eskimo, with Sean behind him. Both of them held flashlights, the giant blinding kind. Zach's light fell on me and I could see his relief.

"Are you okay?" He demanded.

Rio stepped back, but it took a bit of work for Zach and Sean to get through the door. Zach actually shoved at the piled snow, pushing it outside the open doorway and trying to tramp off the boots he wore. Sean stared at Rio, a frown on his face.

"I'm okay," I said. "Just hurt my ankle. Rio was helping me keep warm." I sort of realized then, that I was still in nothing but my undies and the hoodie I'd borrowed. "My clothes were wet," I offered weakly. It did sort of look like we had a little tryst or something. But I didn't think Zach was the sort of guy to judge me.

"Frozen," Sean said as he picked up the stack that Rio had folded for me. "The pants are like ice."

Rio kept his distance. I wanted to reach for him, assure him everything was okay, Zach and Sean wouldn't hurt him, but maybe he wasn't that used to being around people.

"It's best you take him home," Rio said softly. "It's not safe out here."

"Let me get that fire stoked," Zach said. "You don't have any other heat?" He looked around the place and I could tell he was assessing things with that contractor gaze. "My guys are on break but could probably be up in a few days to do some repairs."

"I have no money to pay them," Rio said. "It's fine. Just take Montana home, please. He should be warm and safe, not out here in the wild."

Zach seemed to want to protest again, but Sean touched his shoulder and shook his head. Sean moved to my side and reached out to peel the blankets back over my injured ankle, of which my foot was still sticking out. His examination was similar to Rio's, gentle and thorough. "Not broken," he said.

"Torn ligament," I said. "Rio thinks. He was a combat medic and an EMT." I defended as though Sean was somehow attacking him. Sean took off his coat and handed it to me. "You'll get cold," I protested.

"I'll keep us warm as we walk," he promised. "Let's get you home." He got up and took the flashlight from Zach, who knelt down to lift me. Odd, how Rio was smaller through the shoulders than Zach, but had seemed to lift me easier. Zach straightened and I clung to his neck, worried about my bare legs and the cold. At least it didn't look like the wind was whipping anymore.

"Do you want to take your supplies with?" Rio asked, looking toward the kitchen and the stock of groceries.

"No," I said. "I'll bring you more in a few days. You'll be okay? Keep the fire going? Stay warm?"

"I'm fine," Rio said, not sounding fine at all. He went to the kitchen and handed Sean the empty cooler. "I appreciate the food."

"I'll bring more," I promised as Zach carried me out the door, Sean following. I tried to smile at Rio in assurance, but he closed the door behind us. It hurt a little to have him slam that door closed, like he couldn't get rid of me fast enough. I hoped it was the fact that people were in his space that bothered him, and not me specifically.

Sean pulled a piece of paper out of his pocket, seemed to pretend to draw on it, then handed it to me. Instantly I was warm, even with the wind still swirling some snow around us. "Hold on to that while we make our way back," Sean instructed. "And let me know if you get cold. I'll have to renew it then."

I stared at the paper in my hand. It didn't feel like anything other than paper. "How...?" I had a dozen questions, but Zach's grip on me tightened and we headed down the path, barely visible in the newly fallen snow.

"I won't be able to get your car out yet. Not until they plow the roads," Zach said. "Anything you need from it?"

I never left anything of value in the car. "Some groceries for Rio. It was too much to drag along the path. A few things for the manor."

Odd how fast the trek seemed to be when I wasn't dragging a bunch of food. That fast we were through the trees and I could see my car in the distance, and Zach's truck.

"I'll call my guys. See if we can get some repairs done. No one should live like that," Zach said, sounding angry.

Behind us, a howl broke through the sound of the wind, a long wail of a wolf. Something else I'd learned from the classes at the manor, the difference between a coyote and a wolf. That was a wolf, close too. My grip on Zach tightened.

"Hungry wolves are not good things," Sean said somberly.

"Will Rio be safe?" I asked. "There were wolf tracks near the path to his place. I recognized them from the classes."

Zach kept us moving but looked at Sean. "We'll get him more food," he promised.

But would that keep Rio safe from the wolves? "He's been out here for years," I said more to myself than them. "He knows how to stay safe, right?"

"Sure," Zach agreed. "Let's get *you* home and safe."

"Should I isolate now, you think? Rio didn't seem sick, and no one has seen him in weeks…"

"He won't be sick," Sean said.

"Sounds like food is what he needs," Zach said. "I'll work on it."

"I could use some spiced cider," I said thinking of the blend of spices I had back home. Zach loaded me into his truck, Sean crawling in beside me. The slip of paper Sean had given me had almost completely dissolved. "Is this some kind of psychological thing? To convince my brain I'm not cold?" I held out the last of the fading rice paper for Sean, recognizing it now in the overhead light.

"It's a talisman of warmth," Sean answered.

I squinted at him.

"Psychological," Zach said.

"Weird," I starred at the slip of paper, which vanished moments later. Having used rice paper to cook with a lot in the past, I thought it a bit odd that it dissolved that fast. But it was cold and wet out, so perhaps that didn't help. And I was too tired to push for more answers.

Zach took my keys and moved stuff from my car to the bed of

his truck before getting in and steering us home. The roads were awful, covered in a thick layer of snow there would be no way my car could get through. I could hear the chains on Zach's tires grinding through it and we moved slowly in the dark.

The scent of smoke and Rio still clung to me. Probably the hoodie I wore. I'd have to get it back to him. He probably didn't have a lot of warm clothes. I started to make a list on my phone of things I would need to bring to Rio. Clothes, blankets, food, maybe one of those portable propane stoves.

"That man…" Sean began, but didn't continue.

"He's nice," I said after he was quiet for a few minutes. "Was at the manor for Christmas dinner. Comes to the food bank a lot."

"I hate that we still have a need for that," Zach grumbled. "And worry it's not getting to everyone who needs it."

It didn't. That I knew for sure, which was why I'd brought food to Rio. There were others closer to town that got deliveries from some of the volunteers. I knew there were a handful of the elderly that they checked on too, but the group could only help those they knew about. "I wish we could help everyone," I said.

"How many more are like Rio?" Zach asked.

"What do you mean? Needing the food bank? Or having a house so broken down? I don't know. The people at the food bank might know better. I help refill it every week and it's emptied every week."

We arrived at the manor and the entire cabin of the truck felt like brooding silence. I wasn't sure how to read it. Zach wasn't an overly chatty guy, though he'd always been friendly. And Sean was that very traditional reserved that a lot of Asian people were. I really hoped they weren't judging Rio for his lack of money. Having spent some time in a homeless youth shelter myself, I knew how easy it was to go from something to poverty.

Zach parked the truck in the garage and closed the door on the cold behind us. The garage was a giant thing, big enough to fit at least five cars. Usually, my car was nestled off to the side. I hoped I'd get it back soon.

"I'll get your car towed back tomorrow. Do you have snow tires on it?"

"Snow tires?" I asked. There was a special tire for snow?

Zach shook his head and got out of the truck. He came around the side and held his arms out.

"I can walk," I protested.

"The ground is cold, even here in the garage. Let me drop you off upstairs so you can get your own stuff." Zach waggled his fingers. "Don't be a drama queen," he teased. "Warm is better than frozen toes any day."

I sighed and let him pick me up again. He carried me to the stairs that lead to my apartment over the garage. The stairway was cool, but not cold. He didn't set me down until we were at my door. Sean handed over my clothes, keys, and phone. When I glanced at the time, I realized it was almost ten at night. Crap, I'd really missed the whole day.

"Thanks for rescuing me," I said. "I mean I was safe with Rio, but the cold was sort of intense…" I limped the last few feet to my door and unlocked it.

"Call and get in to have that foot looked at in the morning. I'll drive you down if the roads still aren't clear. Everyone can fend for themselves for breakfast," Zach instructed.

"I can make something simple…"

"Without putting pressure on that ankle? I don't think so. Go rest. I'll see you in the morning." Zach turned away, heading down the stairs with Sean. I sighed and went inside, thankful for the warmth and comfort of my place. It was actually one of three units above the heated garage, since the garage was so large. Mine was a studio apartment, just over 500 square feet, tiny, but felt huge compared to Rio's space. I didn't have a fireplace. Didn't need one as the heat worked great. The garage beneath adding to the warmth. The layout a simple box with the kitchen on one side and the space I'd set up as a living room/bedroom on the other. The thick and cushy furniture, heavy curtains, and plush carpet hadn't really seemed like a luxury when I'd moved in. Compared to the manor with its polished wood floors and detailed crown moldings, the apartment was simple, homey. I had never looked at it and realized how much there really was that I took for granted.

I limped to the bedside dresser area to put my clothes in the hamper and dig out a pair of warm jammies. A hot shower later and I was ready to go to bed. I really hoped Rio was okay. The idea of him alone, in that cold, with very little to eat all winter made me want to drag him to the manor. Zach still hadn't found a gardener. Maybe Rio could do that, make some extra money and not have to be around people.

I laid down in bed and ran through possibilities until sleep took over, washing away anything but memories of being in Rio's arms.

CHAPTER 5

The ligament wasn't torn, thankfully, just stretched the doctor said. The early morning trip to urgent care and some x-rays later, the area was still swollen, wrapped in some immobilizing stuff, but no permanent damage done. The product of twisting my body in a way it wasn't supposed to go. I'd been lucky as it could easily have been a torn ligament and then a broken ankle which would have forced me to stay off my feet for months. As it was, they'd given me a splint with a walking sort of thing that I could fit over a shoe or a boot, but even that had me moving slowly. The splint was slippery and didn't completely remove the pressure from my ankle.

I was preparing lunch in the big kitchen when Zach appeared and handed over my keys. "Car is back. I changed the tires to snow tires, but don't let that fool you into thinking you can drive through piles of snow. A few inches at most. The car is too low to the ground and you'll just bury the undercarriage. I put a shovel in the trunk too in case that happens, but any big drifts and you're stuck."

"Thank you," I said, giving him a big smile. "I need to drop some more stuff off with Rio." I'd made a couple loaves of bread I planned to give him as well as maybe stopping at the grocery store to load up more.

Zach frowned. "You shouldn't be walking that far." But he ran his hands through his hair, which had gotten a little long in the past month or so, and let out a long sigh. "I'll go with you. I want to better assess that trailer in the daylight."

I wasn't sure Rio was going to accept his help. "Can we stop at the grocery store so I can grab him more food?"

"Yeah. But after lunch, okay? Eat and relax for a few." He pointed to my leg. "Off that foot."

"Yes, sir!" I said with a big smile, happy we'd be taking care of Rio. "I got the feeling that you and Sean didn't like Rio. I promise he's not a bad guy."

"I'm sure he's not," Zach said. "He's just..." The pause went on a bit as though Zach didn't know what to say. "Let's just make sure we keep him fed, okay?"

"Sounds like a plan to me."

"Good. Now eat and rest."

Lunch went smoothly, even though my ankle ached from spending too much time on it. By the time we got down to the grocery store, loaded up on supplies, canned goods and the like, plus a giant order Zach wanted sent to the food bank, it was starting to get dark.

Zach pulled an old-fashioned wood sled with iron legs out of the bed of his truck. "Get on. We'll go check on him first. Then you can keep him company while I bring him food."

I marveled at my boss, always thinking ahead. "You're so smart."

"Brilliantly ordinary," he told me as I climbed onto the sled. The air was cold, but no snow was blowing, though the storm from a few days ago had buried enough of the trail that it hadn't been cleared. Too much for Rio to probably do without a snow-blower. There were a lot of other tracks around the trail this time, rabbits, a few birds, and the wolf. I really hoped Rio was okay.

"Fuck," Zach said as we got close to the trailer.

I peered around him, heart thumping with worry that we'd find Rio frozen solid in the snow, but instead it was the sight of the trailer that had him upset. And I couldn't help my gasp either. The weight of the snow from this last storm must have been too much, because the roof was caved in. The back half of the trailer looked like little more than a giant pile of snow, and the section where the fireplace had been was a valley of ice.

"Is Rio okay?" I scrambled to try to get off the sled, ground covered with ice and snow making that impossible. I had to roll to my knees, and get up that way, using my one good leg as support, then limping to the door.

Zach was there first. "Stay out here. I'll look."

My heart hammered in fear. What if Rio was in there? Trapped? Maybe in the back where I knew the bedrooms had been but never seen? If he'd burrowed under his blankets, he could still be alive, right?

Zach had to crawl through the doorway, as the concave roof made it impossible to open completely. He was gone only a minute or two while I clenched my fists and sucked in air, praying. It wasn't like I ever prayed before. Had never been a fan of any god or religion. Self-reliance had been my mantra for a while, and luck. Luck to have met Ms. Yang and gotten this job. Luck that Zach had been a good guy and didn't just fire me and close up the mansion. Luck that I had a safe place to live and enough food to eat. Since the apartment over the garage was part of my pay, and I didn't have to pay rent or utilities, I had a nice nest egg saved up. Maybe I could buy Rio a new trailer? Something with heat and running water? Something safe. And I could cook for him. Make him an official food taster or something.

Please let him be safe.

Zach reappeared looking grim. He said, "It's empty. Blankets and food are gone. Does he have anyone he might have gone to for help?"

"As far as I know, it's just him. He didn't always come into the food bank either. You're sure he's not in there?"

"He's not. And the structure isn't sound at all. Parts of the floor are gone. The section near the fireplace is about all that's standing, and with that roof gone, even that isn't salvageable." He let out a long sigh. "I've been in crack houses with more stable structure than this."

"Not everyone is handy," I pointed out in Rio's defense. "And I don't think he has much money. Just what he gets for being in the military."

Zach carefully searched the area around the trailer, pausing a few times to examine possible tracks. Maybe Rio had a little hut or something, a cave to hide in, anything. Finally, he returned with a frown. "I'm not seeing anything close that can account for where he might have gone."

I swallowed back bile and a curse. "It's so cold, Zach… He can't be out here alone."

"I agree. Let me get you back to the truck, then I'll load up the sled and leave him a note. Hopefully he'll come back to check on things. Get the food and whatever. I'll even leave him the sled."

"We should put him up in the manor. There's room…"

"He might not want to be that close to people, and even if there aren't many around right now, classes restart in a few weeks. It means people in and out." Zach turned an assessing gaze on me. "I'm worried too. But we don't know where he is. Let's leave the food and a note. I'll talk to my guys. The trailer is beyond repair, but I know a guy who deals in trailers. Could probably get something reasonable. It'd cost more to bring a new one all the way through to here than to actually buy something elsewhere." He sighed. "And install solar. He'd have to keep the panels clear, but that would be more reliable and less expensive than a wired line."

"I have money saved," I said. "I can help."

Zach waved at the sled. "Let's get you back to the truck."

"I do want to help," I said, carefully climbing back on the sled.

"Why?" Zach asked. Which I thought was a little rude. Didn't people normally want to help others? "I mean, why Rio? Lots of people you can help through the food bank. Why Rio?"

I shrugged. "No one else seems to care. But he's nice. Lost, it seems. He said he used to be a combat medic and an EMT but doesn't handle blood well anymore."

"That would make things difficult," Zach muttered.

"But does that mean we should throw him away? That seems unfair. I didn't serve my country or do anything to save people's lives, but I sort of have a lot. Why not share it?"

Zach glanced my way, giving me a warm smile. "You're a good kid. No wonder Sofia rescued you."

"I'm twenty-two. Not a kid."

"Mhmm," Zach placated. "And your interest in Rio is completely social, right? Help the veteran? Feed the people? Or because he's kind of attractive and pays attention to you."

I gaped at him. "That's rude."

"Blunt, not rude," Zach corrected. "You're needy."

"I prefer high maintenance," I grumbled.

"I'm not sure about that. Think you mostly are lonely. And that's okay. Life is that way sometimes. Just be sure those you give your interest to, deserve it, yeah?"

"Okay, Dad," I snarked at him. "Tried to give you my interest. Didn't know you had the pretty Asian boy waiting for you."

Zach snorted. "Me neither, but fate surprises us sometimes." We arrived back at the truck and he helped me get in. "Let me load up the sled." He pulled a pad of paper and a pen out of the glove box. "Write him a note. Tell him to come to the manor if he has no place else to go. It's still blizzard season. I hope he's not in some tent out there."

Now that was a horrific idea.

"Write," Zach waved at the paper. "Hurry so I can tuck it in with the food."

I wrote. Given more time, I'd have crafted something better, more convincing maybe. The trek to the manor wasn't a short one. Not on foot. Though I knew as the crow could fly it was probably shorter than taking the winding roads. But I espoused the virtues of the manor, food, warmth, and lots of space, and hoped I sounded convincing enough without being whiny or needy. Zach did not read the letter, at least within my sight. He took it, tucked it in between a stack of cans, then tugged the sled toward the path.

"Turn on the truck," he called back. "Blast the heat, I'll be back in a few."

I reached over to put the key in and turned on the truck, cranked up the heat and shut my door and window. Soon enough the heat began to fog the glass. Was there that much moisture in the air? Did that mean there was another storm coming? I glanced up to the sky, which was darkening already because that's what happened in winter this far north. It could be full dark before five in the evening. But the cloud cover was heavy too. Which worried me.

I pulled out my phone and opened the weather app. The connection was crap, but enough that I got a glimpse of the week's forecast. Cold, colder, and a couple possible snowstorms. I glanced up and stared toward where I knew the trailer would be. Please let Rio see the note and get to safety before another storm hit. How did anyone survive in this sort of weather without heat and warm clothes? Even the short time I'd spent outside had frozen me to the bone through my giant, down feather jacket, knit hat and gloves, and the scarf Ana had crocheted for me. I'd already ordered the Ugg boots I'd been eyeing. Their fur-lined insides looked to be a delightful cure to cold toes, especially since the fake fur didn't stir my inner moral outrage.

Rio could probably use a pair of Uggs. I'd bought them for myself and only agonized about their cost for a few days. Having been a shelter kid for a while, brand names and fancy clothes were on my low value list. Though sometimes spending a bit more made sense. Warmth over pennies, I reminded myself. Unless I was moving to Florida soon, it was a wise investment in my opinion.

The sound of a wolf howl rose from the woods, goosebumps forming on my skin, and the hair on the back of my neck rose. Was Zach okay? He hadn't run into the wolf, had he? I rubbed away the fog on the glass of my window and stared out into the trees, watching for movement, wolf or man. What would we do if we lost Zach? There would be no manor. Sean would probably be heartbroken, perhaps return overseas to his family instead of staying here where people still looked at him funny sometimes.

I'd have nothing… There wasn't enough in my nest egg to buy a house in the New York City, or even rent an apartment near a restaurant where I might work for wages a quarter of what I was paid now.

I trembled, wrapping my arms around myself. How fast everything could be gone. Life was really terrifying sometimes.

Then Zach appeared on the path, slogging through the snow, and my heart flipped over in relief. He made his way to the driver's side and opened the door. He had to shake off a lot of snow before getting in. "I left the sled of supplies close to the door so he'll see it, but away from the normal wind direction. Hopefully it doesn't get buried if we get another storm."

"Did you hear the wolf?" I asked. "Was it close?"

Zach hesitated. "Not too close. Yes, I heard it. Let's get you home and warm. Bet tonight would be a great soup night."

I loved soups and stews and the freshly baked breads that went with them. "Bread is already made. I could do a pumpkin squash soup, or the bacon cheeseburger one you love."

"Hmm, cheeseburger. Sean likes the pumpkin better."

"I can make small batches of both."

Zach nodded and steered the truck back toward the manor. "Let's plan on that, with some of that sourdough Sean likes."

"And pickles for you," I added. Zach loved pickles in his hamburger soup. It was odd, but when I'd tried it, the vinegar touch had been excellent, though not everyone liked it. Zach didn't eat a lot of carbs, part of him being a big guy I think, though he didn't seem to have a weight problem. He was just naturally a bit rounder in the middle.

"I love pickles," Zach said with a straight face. "Of all kinds."

He was teasing now. "Sean's, too?"

"Sean's the best," Zach agreed and winked at me. "And everything attached to him."

I sighed, wanting that for myself. The joy in Zach's expression, his peace when his guy was around, and the confidence that they were it for each other. Zach was right, I was lonely. Sure I hoped Rio might be something, but it wasn't a requirement of me helping him. I tried to think back to my note and hoped I made it clear that we were offering him help simply because he needed it and we were in the position to help. Not because I expected anything from him. But it wasn't like I could change it now. So instead, I pulled out my phone and began planning meals for the upcoming week. It was one of the few things that could relax my anxiety and let me escape from the stress of the world for a while.

CHAPTER 6

A week passed with no sign of Rio. Zach said he was
checking on the trailer, but didn't have much to report
other than it seemed like Rio had taken the supplies we'd given
him. But the news was forecasting the monster of all storms. A
possible three feet of snow, then a clearing up of the sky, which
would remove the cloud cover keeping us in the twenties, and
drop us into the negatives.

The manor was bustling, everyone planning to hunker down.
Zach had checked all the generators, made sure the tractor he
used to plow the drive was full of gas, and commanded that I fill
the pantry with enough food to last a month. That was sort of
normally how it was stocked anyway, except for the veggies
which didn't last that long. But I'd bought frozen and canned, just
in case. And today I was using both of the fancy new ovens to
make rotisserie chickens, a half dozen of them. It would be
enough for sandwiches, soups, and a dozen other things. The
smell was divine, and the warmth of all the fireplaces in the
house going strong made me want to curl up with some cocoa or
mulled cider. Which meant I had both ready in case anyone
wanted some.

Zach came in the side door from the drive as I was pulling the chickens out. He stood in the small mudroom shaking off what looked like a ton of snow. Was it that bad already? I glanced out the window and the flakes were coming down pretty hard, but the view on this side of the house wasn't of much other than distant trees.

"Is it bad?" I asked him.

"I've already plowed the drive twice. The wind is blowing pretty hard, shoving everything I move up against the house. This keeps up all night and it's going to be more than three feet. It will take days for them to clear roads." Zach stripped off his hat which looked like it had been coated in snow and ice. He was wearing one of those full-bodied snow suits that I'd seen some professionals use when battling this sort of thing in the city. The man was prepared for everything, it was what he did. He would keep us safe. Even if the power went off and the snow buried us for a week, he'd make sure everyone was warm, fed, and happy. But it wasn't us I was worried about.

"Do you think Rio will be okay?" My heart did little flip-flops when thinking about him out in this snow.

"I checked his trailer this morning before the snow hit. No sign of new tracks or anyone around. The path hasn't been cleared," Zach said. "Maybe he's with a friend."

"Or found a cave or something to stay in," I said hopefully.

"The mountains aren't that close. They *look* close, but that's a good fifty or so miles. On foot in this snow…" Zach shook his head. "Even if he knew of a good cave, I can't imagine him getting that far, through the woods."

That put a stone in my gut with worry. I bit my lower lip. "Is there someone we can call? To look for him?"

Zach took off his coat and added it to the rack over a drip plate near the door and began stripping off the rest. "I already called the local authorities. Let them know he might be out there. They said without knowing a general area, they won't be able to search. And even then, they would have to wait until the storm was over."

"There's nothing we can do?" I blinked; my vision suddenly blurry with tears. Was Rio out there? Alone? Homeless in the middle of a blizzard, and we couldn't do anything?

"I have a search and rescue spotlight. Was thinking of aiming it out of one of the back windows. You said he's ex-military, he'd be able to follow the light here, or at least get close enough to see the house."

I turned to Zach, hope rising. "Can we? Please. The thought of him out there…"

Zach nodded. "I'll go dig it out of the garage. Keep cooking. Whatever you're making smells amazing. I think I'll be bringing Sean and me into the main house for the night too. Our cabin doesn't have a fireplace in case the power goes out."

"He was in the library," I said. "I brought him a tea tray a little while ago."

"Thanks," Zach said. He shoved his boots off and tiptoed to the opposite edge where everyone now had house slippers waiting. It was a bit of a new thing that had started when Sean arrived. No outside shoes in the house. Everyone had inside slippers. Mine were super cushy with little donuts on them. Zach's had bunnies, which I thought was cute. I knew the cleaning staff loved it because it kept the floors cleaner. I liked how they kept my feet warm on all the cold, hard floors.

He headed out of the kitchen toward the opposite side of the house and the entrance to the garage. I hoped he'd find the light fast and that Rio would see it. No one deserved to be out in this sort of madness.

Once I'd pulled all the meat off the chickens and gotten a pot of soup going, then packaged the rest into the fridge, I washed up and headed to find Zach. Had he found the light? Got it going? Would anyone see it through the storm?

I found Zach and Sean in the ballroom near the fireplace.

They'd made a cozy seating area and I could feel the heat blazing from across the room. "Dinner is almost ready," I told them. "I made chicken noodle soup, so nothing fancy."

"With sourdough bread and homemade noodles?" Zach inquired.

"Of course," I said, because I was a chef and wasn't serving anything out of cans.

Zach snorted a laugh. "Just chicken noodle soup. Not fancy. You realize I've lived most of my life eating the canned stuff?"

"Barbaric," I said dramatically. It had been years since I'd had the stuff. Now I made my soup with real chicken drippings from their roasting process, handmade noodles and always a loaf of crusty bread. It just so happened my sourdough starter had been thriving, so we were living well on the byproducts. "Did you get the light up?"

Zach waved at the back of the house. "I have to keep going out and clearing it off, but it's up. Normally the heat of the light would be enough to keep it clear, but the snow is coming down too hard. I've got a timer on my phone for once an hour."

That wasn't good news. Would he stay up all night?

"It will be fine," Zach promised. "I plan to stay up most of the night to keep an eye on the house. If the power goes, I want the generators up fast. I've already been out clearing them. The wind is blowing snow everywhere. I'll need to build more windbreaks in the spring. And there are a few windows upstairs that I'll need to replace. They are rattling too much for my taste." He pointed to a spot near the back door where he'd set up another drip plate and an old school coatrack to hold his stuff. Everything looked wet. No wonder he was staying near the fire.

I let out a long breath. "Sorry. I can't help but worry."

"I understand. I promise to keep an eye on things. It's my job, right?"

It was. But it was also sort of his personality. I nodded. "Let me get dinner finished up. I'll set up in the formal dining room."

We only used the smaller space when there were no guests, or the party at the house was small, since it fit a dozen at best.

Taking up the task of setting out dinner helped take my mind off worrying about the storm. Ana arrived to set out plates, and began moving bread baskets and silverware. Wind whipped hard enough around the house that I could hear it battering the walls and couldn't help but shiver.

The smell of fresh bread and hot soup gave a little comfort. Everyone began to appear in ones and twos to fill their plates with Zach and Sean arriving last. I ate in silence, listening to everyone talk around me. Zach and Sean didn't say much either, though Zach asked about the storm.

"Is this a normal thing? Like happens every year?" Zach asked Mona, one of the cleaning staff who had been at the manor over ten years. Not all the staff lived on-site, but a handful of us did. Several in the above garage apartments, and another group in a small set of servant rooms on the far side between the garage and main living space. The servant rooms didn't have much more than their own bedroom and a shared bathroom. I was thrilled to have more space than that. Zach had bantered the idea of changing them into a more independent space, but no one wanted that. They thought of the manor as their home, and their rooms were their space in that home, almost a home within a home. That made sense, though sometimes I really liked to get away from the job long enough to recharge. But that was just me.

"We get storms, but usually only a few inches of snow. Can't remember having this much before." She wrinkled her nose. "Not here. When I lived in Cleveland, we got this sort of thing. Lake effect."

Only we weren't anywhere near a lake. Well there was the small lake out back, which was sort of nestled in the trees. But I hardly thought that could stir up this sort of weather.

"It's been an odd weather year," Rico said. He was part of the cleaning staff too, but had only been around two or three years.

"First those storms over the summer making all this weird damage, now these snowstorms. What's next? A hurricane?"

An expression crossed Zach's face that I couldn't read and he glanced at Sean, but Sean was focused on his soup, which he was eating with chopsticks. Sometimes I felt like those two were hiding something. I took another sip of soup, enjoying the rich flavor and the warmth of it, hoping that Rio was either somewhere safe, or headed in our direction so we could keep him safe.

"Maybe the curse isn't broken," Ana said. "Sometimes years would pass before it would show up again."

"The curse is broken," Zach said firmly. "It's more likely this storm is part of the mess of climate change. Or just a really bad nor'easter. I've heard of it happening before."

"I just hope Rio is okay," I said. "Everyone, really." I looked up to find Sean's gaze on me, assessing, but expressionless. He looked away and I felt as though a weight had been taken off me, but I was also done with people for the night. Normally watching everyone eat and enjoy my food energized me. Right now, it made me want to scream that Rio was out there in the cold while everyone else sat here eating and laughing in warmth and comfort.

I picked up my bowl and returned it to the kitchen, beginning cleanup. Ana could finish the rest. I had the strong desire to find the warmest pair of pajamas I owned, and curl up with some cocoa away from everyone. Was I feeling ill? I didn't think so. Just a bit mentally run-down. Not the first time since the pandemic had hit. At the manor we'd isolated enough that right now, with no one visiting, it was almost like normal. No masks, social distance wasn't a big deal, and no one was sick. But out in the world, every time I left the house it was with a handful of masks, hand sanitizer, and a lot of anxiety about the selfishness of other people.

Ana appeared in the kitchen and took over cleanup, shooing me away to rest. I took her up on it and headed to my place, enjoying the quiet warmth of the space. But even after I got into my jammies and slippers with thick socks on my feet, I still didn't feel completely warm. The wind whipped so hard outside that I could almost feel it in my bones. The edge of the chill lingered and I shivered a few times peering out the different windows of my tiny apartment to see if I could glimpse the light, or perhaps Rio on the way to the house. But much like the other side of the house where the kitchen was, my view was of thick trees and not much else.

I tried to watch some things to distract myself. The latest episodes of *Chopped* were unsatisfying. All the holiday baking shows were repeats, and the cycle of fun movies had ended at the beginning of the new year. Reading didn't work either, so I ended up in my tiny kitchen, pulling apart my cupboard to try to inspire something new to cook. I set to making some fancy breads which would require some proofing, but were more than the norm of sourdough. Maybe some French toast would be in order. I had plenty of fresh maple syrup.

In that vein I decided to make a batch of apple cider donuts and snickerdoodles too. Not that anyone at the manor had much of a sweet tooth other than me. I could bring it to the shelter. And on that note, I decided a batch of moon cakes would be a nice addition to our snack plate. Sean had given me a handful of recipes, which I'd spent some time perfecting and now had a dozen little molds to make the tasty red bean or lotus seed cakes. Food could distract me better than most anything else. Even if it wasn't all about eating it for me, but watching others enjoy.

CHAPTER 7

I ended up making a late-night trip to the mansion pantry to refill my rice flour stash. It was almost two a.m., so when I turned to find Zach standing in the door of the kitchen, I almost had a heart attack. With my hand on my chest, I breathed hard and was thankful I hadn't started screaming like crazy.

"Um, serial killers stalk people at night," I said.

Zach smiled. "Know lots of serial killers?"

"None, actually. That I know of. But that's how it works in the movies."

"Shouldn't you be asleep?"

I waved a hand at him and pointed to the rice flour nestled in the bend of my arm. "Couldn't sleep, so I'm baking instead. I am in the process of finishing some moon cakes for Sean."

"I'm sure he'll love them, but maybe you should try to get some sleep?"

"I will, I promise." The wind whipped again, sliding around the house in a howling whine almost like the wolf, yet not. It made me stop and listen hard. "This storm is not letting up."

"It will," Zach promised. "Now, bed. You shouldn't be on that ankle anyway." He pointed to my foot.

I nodded and slowly headed back to my place, not with the intention to sleep, but to finish my baking. One of the perks of being a grown-up was that I could pick my own bedtimes, and eat whatever I wanted whenever I wanted. Downfall was the aftereffects, either exhaustion from lack of sleep or getting chubby from eating too much homemade ice cream. No one ever told you as a kid that grown-ups made bad decisions all the time. Life 101: fuck up but keep going anyway.

Back in my apartment, I resumed baking. Rolled the centers for the cakes and then covered them in the rice flour batter, rolled and shaped them into little treasure boxes with beautifully etched flowers on them. Baked to golden brown, they looked amazing, and I'd already eaten three, so I knew they were good.

My kitchen overlooked the back, right corner of the house, and staring into the trees in the dark didn't seem like much as the snow was piling down, but I found it mesmerizing as I rolled the balls of dough. Maybe I'd make moon cakes for the whole town? Wasn't there a New Year's festival coming or something? When was the Chinese New Year? Would we be celebrating it? Sean didn't seem to associate much with any of the holidays so far, but enough of the manor staff and extended family did. When I looked it up on my phone, it was in February, so we had a few weeks. I'd have to ask about it.

I blinked, pausing in the roll of my hands. Was that movement outside? Well of course there was movement. The snow was still falling, but I thought I'd caught a glimpse of something else. I stared into the woods, more darkness really, as the density of their breadth kept visibility low.

There was something out there, moving slow, careful. I caught a glimpse twice more, something passing the dark trunks of the trees. A large dog? A wolf even? The way it was low to the ground, walking on four legs and pale in color, almost matching the snow made me think wolf before bear or cougar. I set the parts of the cakes aside, covering them in plastic wrap before pulling on my new Ugg boots and coat.

In hindsight it was stupid. No one went out to greet a wolf. But I felt a bit compelled. Needed. The whipping wind did me no favors as I made my way into the tiny hall and down the back stairs to the door out toward the rear of the house instead of the garage. I had to shove the door with all my weight just to get it open.

The pile of snow that had blown up against it made me gasp. Obviously, Zach had tried to keep a lot of the spaces clear, since there was a defined line of shoveled walkway, even if it had another foot of snow on it. And the wind blowing all the snow didn't help. I waded into it anyway, following the path and telling myself I'd have to change pajamas before trying to sleep again. Who needed sleep when there was coffee anyway?

I paused a few times, searching the distance for a sign of movement, and listening for anything beyond the wind. For a moment, an eerie silence descended, like the wind broke and settled, leaving nothing but the falling of a bitter cold.

Okay, coming out into the snow in only boots and a coat over my pajamas, probably wasn't a good idea. I shivered, looked back toward the door a good thirty feet away and wondered what I'd been thinking.

Then I heard a soft sound. A moan or a cry? Faint. But I turned toward it anyway, tromping through the snow, visions of wolf attacks in my brain, but also worried that it was somehow hurt. By morning the temps would be completely negative, and this snow little more than an icy blanket.

I'd gone another twenty or so feet in the woods, snow up to my crotch, legs becoming numb with cold when I saw something. Not a wolf as I had thought at first, but a sled. Piled high with things, like a cooler, a blue bag which appeared to be a tent, and some stacks of canned food. The sled we'd left for Rio?

I ran toward it, heart hammering all while my body screamed at me to go back because we were freezing. When I got to it, I saw him. Curled up with the sled like a wall, shielding him from the cold. Still dressed in nothing more than boots, jeans, and a thick sweater, it wouldn't be enough. How he was alive at all, I couldn't fathom, though when I reached his side, he was warm to the touch though his clothes were soaked.

"Rio…" I called for him, touching his face and turning him to face me. His hair more than wild, and beard badly in need of a trim, he looked like a mountain man. "Rio?"

His eyes opened, that clear blue gaze peering up at me, tired and almost feverish. Was he sick? *Of course, he's probably sick, Montana!* I lectured myself. Out in cold like this? Who wouldn't get sick?

I reached for him, wrapping my arms around his middle and heaving him up with all I could. He was little more than a rag doll. "Help me out a little," I grumbled at him. "David and Goliath here…"

"What do you know of Bible stories?" Rio stuttered as though the cold made it hard for him to speak.

"Lots, sadly. Let's get you warm and worry about my lack of religion later, yeah?" We limped toward the house. At least I could see it. A beacon of warmth, fireplaces gleaming, lights on, even though it was only a handful, and the entrance to the open back door of the garage welcoming. It was the closest. I could have dragged him to the main house, but my place was closer, so to the door and up the stairs, we went. Inside my place I stripped him out of everything and shoved him into the shower, running the hot water up as high as it would go.

I had to return to the lower door and work to get it closed. By then the cold was really getting to me. When I returned to my apartment I stripped as I moved, leaving the wet things in the entry and only grabbing a towel from the closet to wrap around me and a few for Rio. I needed the shower. Heat. Warmth, and now sleep too.

He was curled up in the base of the tub, water flowing over him. Since he wasn't shivering and seemed to be breathing okay, I sucked in a gulp of air, relieved. I put the stack of towels on the top of the toilet near him.

"Can I use some water?" I asked. "Sorry. I need to warm up too."

Rio barely glanced up. Instead, he scooted back a bit so there was room for me. Maybe he wasn't warm enough yet. I'd turn up the heat when I got out. I dropped my own towel and got in, taking over the spray for a moment, thankful for the two shower-heads and the tankless water heater nestled deep within the bowels of the garage. I stood under the spray for a while, letting the feeling burn into me. Nothing looked frostbitten, though I'd felt on the verge of it. And I was so enchanted by the heat and desire to get warm, I didn't realize I was standing with my back to Rio. Meaning he was getting an eyeful of my ass.

Heat funneled into my face. At least that still worked. I reached for my towel and carefully stepped onto the mat to wrap it around myself. Rio's blue eyes were wide and staring at me.

"Are you okay?" I asked him. "The water doesn't go any warmer but I have a lot of blankets." I wouldn't have any clothes that fit him except the hoodie he'd given me. "Let me get your hoodie."

I left him to the shower, turned up the heat, cleaned up the mess of the clothes, stuffing everything into the washer, then retrieving his hoodie. I paused long enough to pull on a pair of underwear, but left the towel in place. When I returned to the bathroom, the water was off. Rio was standing on the mat covered in towels. He looked like a little kid for a minute, eyes huge while wrapped up like a mummy.

I handed him the hoodie. "It's all I have that will fit. Sorry. I turned up the heat, and I have blankets. Lots of blankets. I sort of buy them all the time. I really like the soft ones." The ones that felt like fur even if they weren't really fur. And, I was rambling again. An entire trunk filled with blankets had to be enough right?

Rio took the hoodie and I left him to a bit of privacy, though my mind wanted to cling to the brief memories of being in the shower with him. I sent a text to Zach about finding Rio, and the sled that was out back. Maybe Rio had stuff on it?

I tugged on a pair of warm pajamas, thankful I had a whole drawer of those too. When Rio exited the bathroom, he was in the hoodie with a towel around his waist.

There was a knock at my door which made me jump a half foot in the air. Rio didn't react at all. "It's your boss," he said softly. "Probably wants me to leave…"

I rushed past Rio to the door and opened it to find Zach standing there with a duffel bag in hand. I blinked at him, but Zach wiggled the bag. "For your guest."

"Thanks," I said feeling a bit lost, but it was after three in the morning.

"Make sure he eats. Get some sleep. Ana will take care of breakfast. I'll bring the sled in tomorrow."

I began to protest, but Zach was already on his way back down the stairs. When I closed the door and turned, Rio still stood in the same spot, almost like he was frozen, worried that moving too fast would spook me. Okay so I was easily spooked, but not by him.

"Zach says this is for you." I held the bag out for him. "And I have lots of food. Bacon even. And moon cakes. Lots of moon cakes…" I glanced at the kitchen and the mess, suddenly very tired.

Rio took the bag, but otherwise didn't move.

"I, ah, need to clean the kitchen and maybe get some sleep. There are extra blankets and stuff in that chest." I pointed to the big trunk that I used as a coffee table. "Feel free to eat anything you want."

Rio seemed to suck in air and swallow hard, then he stalked back into the bathroom with his gifted duffel bag in tow. A bit rude, but okay. I had a kitchen to clean.

CHAPTER 8

I worked through the kitchen cleaning and set up food for Rio. I sliced up a loaf of bread and dug out the stack of cold cuts I kept on hand. In reality, my tiny studio kitchen was not as well stocked as the manor. Since I ate most of my meals at the manor, it made sense. Though since the fire earlier in the year that had taken out the kitchen and eventually brought Zach to the house, I'd kept my supplies up a bit more, enough to feed everyone in the manor for a few days at least. If it was coming near its due date, I'd bring it to the manor and use it there. So far, my planning had worked well.

When Rio stepped out of the bathroom in gray sweats and a loose T-shirt, I sort of did a little prayer to everything holy because... um wow, those sweat pants hid nothing, including the fact that he obviously wasn't wearing underwear.

I forced my gaze upward to his face. He'd cleaned up the beard and his hair was pulled back with a hair tie. He looked tired now. A bit on the gaunt side, which made me want to cook something for him, instead of offering sandwiches. But he crossed the room, padding over the hardwood in fuzzy white socks to my side, where he looked longingly at the sandwich tray I'd built him.

"Oh, this is for you," I told him, sliding the tray across the counter. "And fresh bread." I had sliced up a whole loaf of sourdough. "Let me just get the bed ready."

Rio blinked at me, then looked toward the couch, which was a fancy sort of futon. I felt heat rise in my cheeks.

"It's bigger than it looks, I promise. Plenty of room for both of us." I glanced back at the futon. It had always seemed huge to me. But maybe Rio didn't like the idea of having to share a bed with another guy. I really wished I could read him better. "I could sleep on the floor, I guess…" I shuffled across the room to pull the bed out. Though once it was stretched to its capacity, there really wasn't much left of my living room space. I could maybe cram myself in a corner or something.

The pile of blankets stuffed in the chest made a giant mound on the bed. I began laying them out. Most were king-size, since I sort of liked to wrap myself up in them like a burrito. When I glanced back at Rio he was focusing on the food and not my tiny domestic hovel. Maybe he would have been more comfortable in the manor? Though that would have meant waking some of the staff to find bedding and stuff.

Once everything was laid out, I turned back to the kitchen to find Rio's eyes on me. That gaze did a lot of things to me I really hoped he didn't notice. "Um… so…"

"We can share," Rio said. "Just…" he paused as if unsure what to say. "I sometimes have nightmares or trouble sleeping. I don't know how much sleep you'll get."

"Oh. I'm a pretty hard sleeper. Is there anything I can do to help you sleep? I could make you some tea. Sean has given me an amazing blend that zaps me right out."

Rio shook his head. "Having a full stomach helps." He glanced down at the tray and seemed startled to find it empty. He looked away. "Sorry for eating so much."

"Don't worry about that. I have more. Those containers on the counter behind you are full of cookies. And there are probably a couple dozen moon cakes in the fridge. A few blocks of cheese too. The only other meat in there is the uncooked bacon, but I can fry that up for you if you want." I admit it was a bit odd that he'd gone through the two pounds of meat I'd set on the tray, but I could only imagine how hungry he was after being out in this cold for a while. Could he even eat the canned food we brought him? Had it been frozen solid?

I pulled back the blankets on the bed and crawled in, the weight of the pile warm and thick, heaven on my still cold toes. Rio approached slowly, again seeming afraid that he'd startle me. But I patted the spot beside me and reached across to pull up those blankets. "It's a warm nest, I promise. Nothing better on a cold night than lots of blankets and sleep."

He glanced around as he approached. "Do you need me to turn off lights?"

"No, they are on a remote," I said as I picked up said remote from the bedside table. "Do you need something left on?"

He hesitated a minute, glancing at the window, then said, "No."

The blinds were shut, blocking out the bulk of any light that would come through, though I hadn't drawn the blackout curtains. I'd probably regret that in the morning, but if it helped him sleep, I was okay with that.

He crawled in beside me, slow and careful, not getting too close, but curling himself beneath the blankets. I hit the button for the lights, plunging the room into mostly darkness. All I could see was the vague outline of my stuff after my eyes adjusted. But the heat of the blankets and my exhaustion began to tug me down. The side of the bed Rio was on, was the side I normally faced, and I was too tired to change it. He was several inches away, but close enough that I could sort of feel the heat radiating off of him. Was he feverish?

For a few seconds I worried about the ongoing pandemic and if he'd caught it somehow being out in the middle of nowhere on his own, but Zach had ensured we kept up with the science, so I knew that wasn't possible. If he was sick, it would be the cold that had done it. Hypothermia? I didn't know much about it.

"Are you okay?" I asked softly. "Sick or anything? I have some aspirin." Though I recalled he said he ran warm.

"I don't have the virus," he said softly. "Never sick. Not anymore."

"Are you warm enough? I could run over to the manor and get more blankets."

"It's okay, I run warm. Your blankets are nice. Soft. Fuzzy. Sort of like fur."

"It's all fake," I promised quickly. "I'm not into killing animals for that sort of thing…" Probably one of my most awkward bed conversations.

Rio gave the hint of a laugh. "Plastic beasts are okay though."

"I'm all in for recycling. Upcycling too," I agreed.

He gave that husky chuckle again, turning me on in ways my tired brain had no way to really deal with. Fuck, the whole one bed thing was always much sexier in stories. But I didn't think he wanted me all over him. "Are you cold?" he asked.

"My feet," I admitted. "Not as bad as when I got you inside. But that sort of cold lingers. I'll be fine after some sleep."

He rolled over those last few inches, close enough now that the heat of him began to thaw something in my gut I hadn't known had been frozen. He even tucked one of his feet between mine. Warmth began to tug me down to sleep.

"Holy crap you're warm," I sighed. "I'm going to pass out in like two seconds."

"Okay," he agreed. Some of the tension seemed to ease out of him as he lay shoulder touching mine. "Thanks for the food."

"I love feeding you."

He sighed. "I'm always hungry."

"I'll work on that," I promised, my eyes too heavy to stay open.

"It's my curse."

"To be hungry?" I wondered.

"Yes."

"Well you've met the right guy," I told him without opening an eye. "'Cause I'm a chef and love feeding people." If Rio responded I was asleep and didn't hear it.

CHAPTER 9

I woke to the chirping dance of my phone on the bedside table. Technically it was an end table, but whatever. I opened my eyes to glare at it a moment, too warm and sleepy to really want to reach for it. There was an arm around my waist, and a body tucked to mine, spooning me from behind in delightful warmth. My muscles felt like jelly, melted and gooey. I couldn't contain my happy sigh.

No alarm. No anxiety. The idea that Rio had gotten a little clingy in his sleep didn't bother me at all. I hoped it wouldn't freak him out. Though when my phone stopped, then started again thirty seconds later, I began to wonder what the emergency was. Zach had said Ana could handle breakfast. And since I always had the next day's meals prepped, she could have flown through it without help, easily.

Rio began to stir, arm tightening around me, breath hot on my neck. I rolled forward a bit to snatch up my phone and tried not to flinch when Rio seemed to stiffen as he awoke to realize he was holding me. The fact that he didn't immediately jerk away and go flying off the bed made me wonder what was going through his head.

Breakfast outside your door, a text from Zach read. *Make sure Rio eats.*

There was a voicemail too, which I didn't listen to, but thumbed through to the speech to text translation. It seemed to be a ramble from Zach about how food was very necessary for Rio right now. Like I would let anyone starve. Okay so it was after ten a.m., and I'd have to get up and work on lunch for the manor, but after the mass of food Rio had eaten last night, he couldn't still be starving right?

The light through the blinds was bright enough to see the entire room and assure me that either the storm was over, or the sun had peeked through the trees. That meant it would be cold. A hot lunch would be a must.

I sent a text back to Zach letting him know we'd eat and be over soon, then put the phone back on the nightstand.

"You okay?" I asked softly.

Rio was silent for a minute or so, seeming to just breathe, but finally said. "I slept pretty well."

"That's good, right?"

"I can't recall sleeping more than an hour at a time. Not in years."

That sounded terrible. "I'm sorry."

"No reason to be. Not your fault." He sucked in another long breath of air. "I smell food."

I sniffed but didn't smell anything. "That's a powerful sniffer you have. Zach says breakfast is outside the door. That's what the noisy phone was about. I'll have to get up and head over to start on lunch too."

Neither of us moved for another minute or so.

"You okay?" I asked him.

"Thinking."

"Is that good or bad?"

"Not sure yet." Rio slowly pulled away. I instantly missed the warmth of him. I sat up and turned his way, not sure what to say, but he was staring at me with a bit of wonder.

"What?" I asked. He shook his head, though there was a bit of a curve to his lips, like he was trying not to smile. I reluctantly slid to the edge of the bed and got out, making my way to the door. Surprisingly the basket sitting on my welcome mat was huge. How much did Zach think we needed?

When I went to lift it, I discovered I needed two hands. "Wow, Zach must think we're hungry," I joked as I dragged the basket inside. In the kitchen, I began to unpack it, finding an entire container of the chicken I'd made yesterday, a dozen hardboiled eggs, an entire pound of fried bacon, and a dozen sausages, as well as a container of fresh cut strawberries and two thermoses of coffee. Wow that was a lot of food.

It was only as I was setting the empty basket beside the door, that I realized the two containers of cookies I'd left on the counter from the night before, were empty and sitting in the sink. Had Rio gotten up and eaten them all? He still hadn't moved from the bed, though he wasn't looking in my direction.

He said he hadn't slept more than an hour at a time in years, I assumed until now, but had he slept much? "How long did you sleep?"

"Only got up once. Sorry I ate all your cookies."

"I can make more. Come eat," I told him. "Looks like they packed plenty of food. I sort of eat like a bird in the morning myself. Zach complains that I drink more coffee than someone my age should, but I tried tea in the morning, and it's just not the same." I glanced at the thermoses. "I can make you tea if you prefer. I have a lot of blends. Sean creates the blends himself."

Rio rose slowly, stretching, which pulled his shirt up a bit and I tried to pretend it didn't give me something to drool over. He made his way over, looking at the spread, which would have been enough food to feed the entire manor staff, and seemed to focus on the bacon. I pushed it his way.

"I'm going to jump in the shower. Eat. I'll be out in a few, then you can have the bathroom, okay?"

"Are you going to eat any of this?" he asked.

I took a single piece of bacon. "Just leave me some coffee and I'm good."

He stared at me like he thought I was crazy, but didn't say anything more as I made my way to my dresser, picked out some clothes and then headed into the bathroom. I hoped Ana had made bread already for the day, as they'd only need to be popped in the oven. If Rio's appetite kept up this way, I'd have to substantially increase the meal size I was making. It wasn't a big deal; just meant I might need a trip to town sooner than I had planned.

I got in the shower wondering how he could still look gaunt when he was stuffing himself with pounds of food. Some sort of illness? A ridiculously high metabolism? Not that it mattered, I'd cook for him anyway. How sad it would be to have that sort of issue and be food insecure. It made my heart hurt at the thought. He was always hungry, he said. I hoped I could fix that. If not, what kind of chef was I?

When I got out of the shower, cleaned up and dressed, returning to the main area, Rio had finished the entire spread of food, even going so far as to wash all the dishes by hand.

"I have a dishwasher. You didn't have to handwash all that."

He shrugged, looking a little sheepish. "Habit."

That made sense since who knew how long it had been since he'd had power. "Bathroom's free. Did Zach leave you other clothes?"

"He brought my stuff up from the sled while you were in the shower," Rio said and pointed to a bag at his feet. His cheeks turned a little pink. "He had the staff wash them first."

That was nice of Zach, though I could understand why Rio was embarrassed. His things probably hadn't been washed in a while. "That's great. Means you have your own stuff to wear, right? You're probably more comfortable in your own things."

"He left me some new things too," Rio said quietly staring at the bag at his feet.

"Zach is very thoughtful that way. Probably wants to make sure you're warm." I waved at him to head to the bathroom. "Get ready for the day, I've got to run over and start lunch in a few."

"I should go," Rio began, looking away.

"Go where? Were you staying with a friend? We were at your trailer. Zach says it's damaged beyond repair."

Rio blinked and wouldn't meet my gaze. "I don't want to be a bother."

"You're not. Did Zach say you were a bother?" He wouldn't. I knew he wouldn't because that wasn't who Zach was.

"No…"

I smiled, instantly relieved. "Good. Then go get dressed. I can't wait to show you my kitchen." Rio's gaze flicked at the little kitchen I was standing in. "Not this," I said, waving a hand at the tiny space. "My kitchen. The kitchen of my dreams, where batches of bread are born and the smells of heaven surround me all day."

Rio's lips twitched again, like he was fighting a smile. "You really like to cook, don't you?"

"Yes, sir," I said giving him a mock salute. "It's my mission in life. To feed the hungry with tasty goodness. Just tell me what your favorite foods are, and I will make it happen."

He glanced at the empty containers seeming to gulp. "The strawberries were good. Haven't had fresh fruit in a long time. It's not usually at the food bank more than once or twice a year. And I need a lot of protein, so I have to focus on that…"

"Okay, fresh fruit I can do. And protein. No need to pick and choose right now. The manor is stocked." I began making mental plans of the things I would make for him. I wasn't sure how much fresh fruit there was at the manor, and if the roads took a few days to clear, we had plenty of preserves and cans. But I could make it all taste amazing.

He stared at me a moment longer, and I wondered what sort of thoughts were going through his head. "Thank you for feeding me."

"Of course."

He reached out and touched my face. Just his palm on my cheek, like he couldn't believe I was real. "Sorry about..." he pointed to the bed. "You don't need me all over you."

I laughed. "Um, you can be all over me if you'd like. I'm not opposed. Not sure if you've looked in the mirror in a while, but you're pretty hot."

He frowned. "I have nothing to offer you."

"Why would that matter? I'm not looking for a sugar daddy." A Daddy on the other hand... and hot damn did Rio fit that. I glanced at the kitchen, hoping he didn't think I was going to require anything for all the food he'd received. Too many years had passed since my time on the streets. I'd forgotten some of the old rules of exchange.

"You're not required to be into me," I told him. "Not for food, or shelter, or anything. I really do want to help. Me thinking you're smoking hot does not mean we have to be anything."

"Smoking hot?" He smiled a little. "I'm too old for you."

"Pfft, I like my men seasoned."

"Like your bacon?" He inquired. "Bit of pepper and jalapeno?"

"You got all that? No one at the manor appreciates the subtlety of it, but I make pork belly into bacon. Smoke and flavor it myself. Used to buy it at a butcher but the flavors were too strong, or they would use too much wood and it would taste like tree bark."

"The bacon was excellent," Rio assured me. "The chicken too."

"Hot damn. I love when a man loves my cooking. You're not allergic to any of that are you?"

"Only thing I'm allergic to is chocolate..." he paused as if debating whether to add something else. I quirked a brow at him. "Wolfsbane, too. It's in tea sometimes."

"The chocolate thing is sad. I have some great chocolate recipes, and I will watch the tea blends. But I'm sure I can keep you full without either of those things."

"I don't understand why you would care."

"Food allergies are a big deal," I told him. "In culinary school I took a bunch of classes on dietary science about allergies and how they affect everything from immune deficiencies to entire populations based on shifts in the nutrient supply. Fascinating stuff."

"I don't mean the allergies. I mean, why me? You have people here already to feed."

"Why not? Everyone deserves food."

"I'm cursed," he said quietly.

"Poverty is a bit of a curse. People think they are immune, but it's one bad turn to drop most of us in that pit. Been there myself. Sometimes you really need a hand up to get out of it. But you gotta be willing to accept the help. Just understand I want to help, not because you owe me anything, you don't. I would help everyone if I could."

"Even if they weren't hot?" Rio seemed to mock himself with that statement.

"You are hot," I shrugged. "But I work at the food bank. I see a lot of people in hardship. I wish there were less people in need. The pandemic has made it worse. I'm not a medic or a scientist or an economist. All I can do is feed people."

"That's important too," he said softly.

"It is," I agreed. "Now I need to get ready for the day. Lots to prepare. And I have to see if Zach thinks the roads will be clear enough to get to town soon. I try to deliver fresh baked goods to the food bank at least once a week. If you're not opposed to helping a bit, I could use a hand making up bread."

"Never made bread before."

"Lots of kneading." I glanced at his hands, long fingers, big hands, and tried not to think about the delightful things they could do to me, and imagined how I could teach him to work a bit of dough. "Willing to help?"

After a moment, he nodded.

"Off you go then." I shooed him toward the bathroom.

Rio stared at me another moment or two before he made his way to the bathroom, still silent. I wasn't sure if it was brooding or he simply thought that hard, but it was okay, he didn't need to be a *Chatty Cathy* for me to feed him.

After the door closed, I dried all the dishes and tucked them back into the basket to bring back to the manor with us. Zach sent me a text that read, *Did he eat?*

Of course, I sent back. I thought for a minute or two about asking the question but sent it anyway. Zach was older than me, a good twenty years or so, I thought; that meant he knew more right? I suspected Rio was at least a decade older, but couldn't be sure. Since I had a thing for older men, the number didn't matter so much. *He ate it all. A lot of food. Do you think he's sick?*

The little bubble appeared for a while, but all I got back was *No, not sick.* At least that was a relief. Wasn't there some sort of illness that made people eat and eat and eat until they died because they didn't have the "full" off-switch? I thought I'd seen some show about it a while back. But wouldn't that mean Rio would have been larger rather than looking like he barely ate?

I tugged on my shoes and frowned at the worn pair that had appeared next to mine on the mat beside the door. Obviously Rio's, since they were filled with holes and worn down, I didn't know how they could be useful at all in the snow, or even if the weather had been nice. I'd find him a pair of slippers for in the house, something soft with solid bottoms. There were a dozen sizes in the entry closet for guests.

When Rio emerged, it was in a pair of worn jeans, a dark T-shirt, and what appeared to be a newish sweater over the top that was a little large on him. Must have been Zach's, since Rio was leaner than my boss. The socks were obviously new too, as they were crisp and white. His long hair was pulled back in a little ponytail. I smiled. "You look great. Ready to see my kitchen?"

This time he did smile. "Take me to this wonderland of yours. I'd like to see where bread is born and cupcakes rise from the soil."

I laughed at his teasing. "If you like cupcakes, I can make some crazy good cupcakes. No one at the manor really eats a lot of sweets, and I'm not technically a pastry chef, though I had a few classes. It's more a hobby, but I'd love to finally have someone to bake for who enjoys it." I pointed to the empty cookie containers. "You must have liked those."

He flushed and looked away. "They were delicious. Those moon cake things were good too, though different… the texture was a bit unexpected."

"I forgot about those." But the containers hadn't been in the sink. I opened the fridge and retrieved one of the containers. Either he hadn't liked them as much or the cookies had filled him up. "Sean likes these the most. And Mr. Yamamoto, but I don't think he'll be up for a few days since the snow is so bad." I added the container to the stack and wondered how I'd get it all over to the house. Rio lifted the whole pile as though it were nothing. He was wearing his worn-out shoes now.

"Thanks!" I told him as I stepped out the door and held it for him. He followed. "We'll get you a pair of slippers when we get to the manor. Sean doesn't like outside shoes worn in the house."

Rio didn't protest, just followed me down the stairs and through the garage. His sled full of supplies had been pulled inside and left near the doorway to the stairs, but Rio didn't more than glance at it. I hoped he'd remain at the manor a few days at least, maybe let us work out a safe place for him to stay since his trailer was ruined.

CHAPTER 10

I found him slippers and showed him to the kitchen, which was sparkling clean because Ana knew I loved everything spotless before I began cooking. Rio seemed a bit dumbfounded at the size of the kitchen, which was easily at least twice the size of my apartment.

"I've never been in a kitchen this large. You do all the work in here yourself? You must be running miles a day just to get from one end to the other."

That was a bit of an exaggeration, though when we had guests sometimes it was a bit maddening. "For parties I have help. Most of the time it's me and Ana. She'll be off helping the cleaning staff, but will probably be back for dinner prep." I put all the dishes away and began pulling out supplies for lunch. Since Rio liked my bacon so much, I grabbed a bit more of that to make. Lunch would be fried chicken and stuffed potatoes. Not fast at all, but filling. Dinner for the manor would be easy enough to shift to a salad spread with the leftover chicken. My planning on nonbusiness days was a bit looser. Though I had a set schedule of proteins, which was written out on a chalk board on the far wall for everyone to see. Red meat twice a week, fish twice a week, and the rest filled in with random other things, chicken, turkey, pork, and the occasional processed meat like hot dogs. Though that was more of a summer thing.

I texted Zach the change and got a thumbs-up affirmative. Then sent him a question about the snow. He didn't respond to that. From the blue sky and bright light that I could see from the window, the snow was done, but I suspected the cold would be intense. I could get by without leaving the house today, but would have to get out tomorrow if I wanted fresh bread sent to the food bank.

"What do you want me to do?" Rio asked.

"Ever cut up whole chickens before? Fresh but already dead, I mean. It's not like we have to catch them or anything."

"I have not, but if you show me what to do, I will do my best."

Estimating by how much he'd eaten last night and this morning, I decided to triple the amount of chicken I needed. "To the freezer we go. You can help me juggle chickens."

He smiled and shook his head a little, but followed.

Rio was actually a really good assistant. He listened attentively. Was a bit shocked about defrosting chickens and how I had a microwave that was fancy enough to estimate the weight and defrost them in minutes. He took to being a sous-chef easily, cutting up the chicken, helping me dredge it in eggs, cream, and a spiced flour mixture. He was amused by the elaborate splatter shield and apron combo I had for frying, and worked on kneading bread while I cooked the chicken.

We baked potatoes smothered in olive oil and course sea salt, then cut them open to spoon out their filling into a bowl to mix with broccoli, bacon, a homemade ranch dressing, and pickles, then put them back in the oven. "The pickles seem an odd addition. And weren't homemade," Rio remarked. "Everything else you make?"

"I don't use pickles a lot. Tried to can them once, but they ended up too salty. I get most of the preserves from people in town during the summer. Only bought two jars of pickles from them this year, so they are already gone. I will plan better next year." The chicken was looking amazing and I was finally getting hungry. The smell of the twice baked potatoes was a dream of comfort food. "I like to know what's in everything. If I know what's in it, I can remake it."

"That sounds a bit magical," Rio admitted.

"Not as magical as you making perfect loaves of bread like you've done it a thousand times. It took weeks for me to perfect the roll." I pointed to the rack of bread ready to go in the large stand proofer Zach had installed for me. "We used to tease each other in culinary school that those who mastered it were meant for big things, the rest were meant for McDonalds. People didn't stay in school if they couldn't get through the basics."

"I think my years as a medic helps. Lots of precision in that," Rio said. "I'm out of practice, but it's nice to be useful." He looked around the space, "And you have so much room without other people around." He flushed and looked at me. "I mean like crowds, not you."

"No worries. I understood. Let me get out some serving stuff so we can get everything out for lunch."

Rio tensed.

"You don't have to eat with the group if you want. You can eat in the kitchen." I pointed to the small corner booth that Zach had put in at my request just a month earlier. Sometimes even I needed a break from all the bustle of things.

"Thank you. Let me help with your trays at least."

Lunch setup was easy. Two giant warming trays, a salad with a selection of dressings, and the moon cakes, all arranged on a small table in the large ballroom area. Normally, if there were guests, the tables would be spread across the distance of the room to keep everyone separate and the windows would be open to let in the breeze. Though with the current piles of snow sloped against the back of the house, that would have been a chilly breeze. I could see the path out the back and the main patio appeared to be cleared. Zach likely had carved a path to his cabin as well.

Rio loaded the giant warming platters onto the table like they weighed nothing, and I put out a pot of hot water for Sean's tea, as well as filling the coffee maker. Rio's gasp made me turn, almost dropping a stack of cups thinking he'd hurt himself. But it was Sean standing a few feet away that seemed to have startled him. The man did walk very softly.

"Sorry," Rio said, bowing his head a little and taking a step back.

Sean waved his hands and gave a slight smile. "I apologize for startling you. Please sit and have something to eat."

"Montana said I could eat in the kitchen," Rio said quietly.

I jumped in to try to ease a bit of the tension. "We'll eat in the kitchen today," I told Sean. "Rio is adjusting to being around the bustle of the cooking life, and he needs a bit of a break. He's been really helpful with lunch prep." Not that I thought Sean would do or say anything bad, although I couldn't help but worry that Rio would take something the wrong way.

Sean nodded. "Be sure you eat," he told Rio. "That is all that's important." His gaze seemed to glide over Rio, assessing.

"I've been feeding him," I promised. "I've only had a day to feed him up." I felt defensive of the fact that Rio still looked thin. But that wasn't something fixed in a single day.

The back door opened, letting in a giant fist of icy air. Zach stepped inside, shaking off a ton of snow and the cold. He shut the door and began stripping layers.

"That smells amazing," he said. "Will you be eating with us, Rio?"

Everyone was very intent on Rio eating, and Rio looked a bit like a caged tiger in that moment, starving but wanting away from everything.

"I'm going to take Rio to eat in the kitchen," I said. "I want to keep an eye on the bread." Not that it would do much in the proofer while I was away from it, but it sounded like a good excuse. "Will we be able to get to town tomorrow to drop off bread for the food bank?" I hoped I'd be able to get some supplies too, like fresh fruit for Rio.

"Sure. I've been out helping the county plow some of the smaller roads, and people's driveways as I can. Snow is done, but the wind is still high and blowing everything around. And that cold is brutal. It's negative four out there, and that's not accounting for the wind chill." Zach looked at Rio. "You should probably plan to stay here at least a few days."

"I don't want to be a burden," Rio said quietly.

"You're not," Zach said. He glanced at Sean, but then back at Rio. "Just be sure you eat as much as you need. The house is stocked, and Montana is an excellent chef."

I looked back and forth from Zach to Sean, wondering what the obsession with Rio eating was. Yes, he was thin, but it wasn't like he was suddenly going to go raving mad and eat *us*. "I promise to keep him fed." I put my hand over my heart, like I was vowing to care for a puppy we'd found in a ditch or something. It felt a little silly, as Rio was a grown man. But I wanted to take care of him.

Zach nodded and gave me a warm smile before making his way over to Sean, who accepted a soft kiss on the lips before they both made their way to the table for food. "Let me get the fire stoked," Zach told Sean. "We'll sit over there. I know how much you hate the cold." He pointed toward the corner near the fireplace.

I took Rio's hand and tugged him toward the kitchen. I'd left two whole chickens and a dozen twice baked potato halves for Rio. Would he eat it all? It was okay if he didn't, as long as he was full, that was all that mattered.

He hesitated as he watched me put a single chicken leg and a twice baked potato half on my plate and head to the corner booth. I waved at the counter. "Eat. Let me know if you need more."

He stood there a few moments longer before picking up a plate and filling it with food. I didn't remark on the volume, or even try to focus on it at all. Instead when he sat down, I turned our conversation toward dinner, and the idea of making a fruit tart for dessert.

CHAPTER 11

"I've never seen stuff made from scratch like this before," Rio remarked as I whisked the custard on the stovetop for the tart. "Pudding comes in a box."

"Yuck. You'll never go back once you've tasted mine," I promised him. "That stuff in a box is not even close to this real custard cream." Normally I'd have made it a chocolate custard with melted chocolate folded in, but this was a delicate vanilla cream, with real vanilla bean. It would be light and decadent with fruit on top.

"I get lots of boxed stuff from the food bank," Rio said quietly.

I instantly wanted to kick myself. "Sorry. My privilege is showing. I've been homeless. I should know better."

"You were homeless?"

"Yeah. Folks kicked me out for being queer. Like somehow it was a surprise. I'm a very obvious queer, always have been. I'm the swishy kind of queer that insecure men try to warn the world about." I waved my hand about.

"Queer," Rio said, sounding amused. "I've always found that word funny."

I paused and glanced at him, "Did you just make a pun? Oh my God, you did!"

His cheeks turned pink, but he laughed. "Sorry, not laughing at your misfortune."

I shook my head. "No worries. It's in the past. I mean it's always a worry. If Zach hadn't been so amazing when he took over the house I might be back there. But he pays us well. I have a little nest egg saved up just in case. Though I can honestly see myself working here forever. I just hope this pandemic ends soon so we can have more than a handful of people in the house at a time."

"You guys did great over the holidays, keeping everyone safe while still having people in. I can't remember the last time I had a holiday meal. And the food was fantastic."

I could feel myself glow at his comment. A pure joy glow. Wow, it had been a while since I'd felt that sort of pride. "I worked really hard to make it diverse."

"I tried everything," Rio admitted. "Well, anything that wasn't chocolate."

"There were a lot of chocolate in the desserts. I'll make sure to add different stuff to the dessert table next time. There's more than just cookies and pie."

"Cookies and pie are good. Though this tart thing smells amazing," Rio said as he stood beside me.

"Whisk this for a moment while I prepare a cooling bowl."

He blinked but took the whisk. His strokes weren't as even or practiced as mine, but he'd keep it from burning just fine. I filled a bowl with ice, and then set another on top before putting the tart tin next to it, the crust already baked and ready for filling.

"This is a bit of magic," I promised him as I took the whisk and turned off the stove before carefully taking the pot by the handle. "Watch." I whisked as I slowly poured the filling into the iced bowl, and it began to thicken, looking creamier with each chilling pass. "Can you grab me a spatula?" I asked.

He glanced around and then pulled one from the container near the stove, handing it over.

"Thank you, kind sir," I said flicking the whisk on the side of the bowl and handing that over before taking the spatula. The last part was a gentle fold, ensuring everything was evenly chilled, heat mostly gone and the thick creamy goodness ready for the shell.

"It is a bit of magic. This will have to go in the fridge?"

"This will have cooled it enough so I can put the fruit on, then put the whole thing in the fridge."

Rio had done a good job cutting up a stack of fruit into fine slices and sprinkling them with lemon juice to keep them from browning. Mostly berries, we had a few kiwis, and enough straw-berries, raspberries, and blackberries to make the tart an artfully delicious treat. I carefully layered the custard into the tart shell, scraping the bowl and smoothing the top. The tart itself sat on a cookie sheet with a layer of ice spread across it. Quick and easy. I had a lot of hacks I'd learned in culinary school. The tart that would have taken most places half a day to create and chill, would take less than a half an hour for me.

After I smoothed the top of the custard, I licked the spatula. "Oh my God, it's so good. Try this," I held the spatula out to Rio.

He hesitated a moment before taking it and trying a bit. His eyes widened.

"Good, right? I mean it will be even better cold and fully set up with the pop of the fruit and glaze, but yum…"

"I expected it to be sweeter, but this is perfect." He took another long lick of the spatula. "Thicker than sweet cream, but not really vanilla pudding. Doesn't have that weird aftertaste or super sweetness."

I smiled at him, and began layering the fruit across the top. The chilling of the cream making it firm enough that the fruit wouldn't sink. "Magic," I told him.

"Indeed." He reached out to touch my bottom lip, his thumb

brushing across it and my pants suddenly tightened. His thumb came away with a touch of cream.

"Must have missed that," I said quietly as he licked his thumb and I imagined him licking other things. I couldn't stop from licking my lips and sucking my lower lip in my mouth, worried I'd made more of a mess of myself.

Rio's gaze fell to my mouth and he sucked in air, like he was startled by something. It was an odd moment, like the sort you see in movies and read in novels, about being caught in a web of emotion. Desire, first and foremost, then a bit of worry that something was being misread. Did Rio feel the pull I felt? Was it just wishful thinking? Was he really looking at me like he could eat me? Kiss me stupid? And holy fuck wasn't that hot?

I had a long moment of being caught in his gaze, unsure what to do. Worried that any move I made would be wrong.

But it was him who leaned forward, fingers on my chin, tilting my face up to meet his kiss. A soft touch of lips, the delicate dance of his tongue tracing the outline of them, as though searching for more custard, and me opening to him. The kiss expanding into something hungry and sensual. He tasted of the custard and the warm mulled cider I'd prepared and kept going all day. Rio's mouth, firm on mine, was a bit of heaven.

It was a fight not to reach out and touch him, but my hands were covered in fruit juice, and I worried I'd scare him away, even though he had made the first move. We stayed like that for a moment. His intense blue gaze focused on me, lips on mine in a sweet dance of small kisses and warm breath. I had a thousand questions, and only one real desire.

The sound of the door opening behind us made Rio take a step back. I knew it was Zach by the sound of his snowsuit rustling. Heat flooded my cheeks. Had I just been making out with Rio in the kitchen while I was supposed to be working? Crap.

I turned back to the fruit, madly putting them on the tart in perfect layers and trying to steady my breathing. Facing the island meant no one could see the erection straining my too tight pants. Maybe I needed to start wearing something looser around Rio. As if I owned anything not fitted.

"How's everything going?" Zach asked from his spot in the doorway.

"Dinner's in process," I promised. "Rio's been a big help."

"We have a Caesar chicken salad with fresh rolls for dinner, right?" Zach wanted to know. It had been what I texted him earlier. "And soup."

"Yes," I agreed.

"And a fruit tart?"

I glanced down at it. Okay so the fruit tart didn't really go with salad and soup. "Rio said he doesn't get much fruit."

"Of course," Zach said, sounding a bit amused. "Since all you have left is the soup, perhaps I can borrow Rio to help me haul wood in for the fireplaces?"

Rio half jumped away from me. "Sure. I can help."

"He needs snow gear," I reminded them both.

"On it," Zach promised. Rio glanced back at me, something in his eyes I couldn't quite read. But he'd kissed me first, so I hadn't been imagining that. Had Zach seen? Was he mad? Was that why he was pulling Rio away? But that made no sense. Zach was never mad. Cautious, but never angry.

"Thank you for your help with dinner," I told Rio as he followed Zach to the mudroom closet. He'd helped prep the chicken, and cut up the salad as well as shape rolls I had yet to bake.

"You're welcome," Rio said.

Zach dragged Rio away to help him load firewood. Which meant I missed his presence pretty fast. Odd how I'd worked mostly alone for over a year and never been bothered until now. Ana and I had never been overly chatty. Not that Rio was either. It was more the idea of his awe over the fresh flavors and foods he hadn't ever had, or hadn't experienced in years. I needed to change up the menu more. Find things that wowed people, even if it was the staff. That's what kept me motivated. Though Rio's admiration was a bit more than simple food prep. I'd cook anything for him if he kept kissing me like that.

CHAPTER 12

I worked on dinner, filling the house with the delightful smells of baked bread and cinnamon rolls. The fruit tarts were in the fridge. I planned to take one back to my apartment later with Rio so he had snacks overnight. And I made a dozen more hard-boiled eggs, and even some prosciutto wrapped cheese sticks. He had said he needed a lot of protein. My shopping list was expanding, but I would make do with thawing racks of ribs if I needed to.

When Rio came back in from their adventure in refilling the manor's many fireplace wood stores, he stripped out of his gear and was more than a bit sweaty underneath. "I should shower," he said quietly, standing in the mudroom. "Zach said they could find a room in the house for me."

"Sure. If you don't want to stay with me." I agreed, wondering if he just wanted space, or if being stuck with me annoyed him. I did tend to talk a lot while cooking, telling stories about a particular dish and how I'd learned to make it, or discovered a better recipe.

"I don't mind staying with you. Just don't want to be a burden."

"You're not. I enjoyed having your help today. And knowing you like the meals I'm preparing makes me feel like a little kid on Christmas morning. Nothing makes me happier than when someone likes what I cook."

"I eat a lot of food," he said sounding a bit sad.

He did eat a lot. More than anyone I'd ever met. Couldn't imagine it was still from starving as he'd have to get full sometime. "I meant to ask about that. I mean, not like intrusively. But just that, are you okay? There's not a free clinic in town." I was suddenly wondering if there was a way to fix that, "But I know of a few in the city. I could drive you down…"

"It's nothing modern medicine can fix." He breathed out a long sigh. "It's more of a curse."

"I'm sorry. I promise I don't mean to pry. Eat as much as you need. I love to cook. I hate to think of you in any sort of distress."

He was quiet for a moment, staring at me as he hung things up to dry. "I can't remember the last time I was satisfied for more than a day or so."

"Maybe Zach can find work for you here. We've needed a gardener for a while, someone to help him with outside maintenance. I would keep you well fed." I liked the idea of Rio being here, safe, and close to me.

"Not sure I'm a good fit. I'm not good around people." He looked away.

"You do okay around me." Maybe crowds were more of a PTSD issue. Right now, we didn't have large groups at the manor. And even those were staggered with lots of cleaning in between. No gatherings of more than five really. Not until the pandemic was over. Zach was nothing if not overly cautious. Currently, with only the staff in residence, life felt a bit normal. Those who used to drive in each morning, some of the teachers, event coordinators, and even Mr. Yamamoto who managed a lot of the manor paperwork, were all on winter break. I knew Mr. Yamamoto was still doing a bit of work from home, though Zach insisted he take time off. He had a new grandchild to spoil, so it hadn't seemed any sort of hardship.

I'd gotten used to making him a very traditional breakfast over the past year. I hoped he was safe and getting much needed family time. "Zach doesn't interact with the guests much either. But we'll be closed another two weeks. New class schedule picks up in February."

"I don't know much about gardening," Rio said.

"Not much gardening to do right now with five feet of snow on the ground," I pointed out. "I think you'd do a lot of what you did today. Fill firewood, maybe shovel snow."

Rio glanced back at the door. "Zach showed me how to use the tractor."

"Really? I've wanted to try that thing out. It's crazy cool." Since the circular drive was so large, Zach had decided that instead of using the plow on his truck to try to clear it, he had a snow tractor delivered. Apparently, it was something he had in storage for his construction business, but rarely used it as they did mostly internal renovations during the winter. It looked like a mini-Cat with a safety glass enclosed cabin. It couldn't clear the drive as fast as the large plow on Zach's truck, but the tractor left cleaner lines, and less ice trails he'd have to break through. "Was it fun?"

"Intense…" He seemed to think about it. "But yeah, a little fun." He looked down at himself. "It was hauling the wood that did this." He waved his hands at himself. "I thought I stocked up on wood at my place, but the pile here is huge."

I nodded. "Zach had it shipped in before the leaves began to turn. Anything they cleared off a work site, and then more. He wanted to be prepared in case the power went out and the generators didn't do enough. He's sort of the king of being prepared for anything."

Rio looked away. "I can see that about him."

"Anyway. All your stuff is up in my place. Why don't I walk

RECIPE FOR A CURSE

you up so you can shower? I'll call Ana to look after the kitchen for a bit. You can get cleaned up before dinner. That way you don't have to decide if you want to stay with me or not until later. And I can grab a bit of a break."

Rio hesitated a moment, then nodded. "I get the feeling you don't take a lot of breaks."

"Busted," I teased as I sent Ana a text and got a reply back that she was on her way down. Not much for her to do as it would just be sliding the rolls into the oven twenty minutes before dinner. But I felt better when the kitchen was under control. "I'm a bit of a workaholic." I crossed the kitchen and slid his house slippers his way. "Or you could say I get a lot of breaks because cooking is a lot of hurry up and wait. Let's get you cleaned up." That phrase sounded more PC in my head than it did out loud.

Rio stepped into the slippers and followed me across the kitchen and toward the opposite garage door. Once we reached my apartment, there was a paper bag sitting outside the door. When I glanced at it, it appeared to be filled with clothing. More T-shirts, sweats, socks, and even an unopened pack of boxers.

"Looks like Zach left you a gift," I said as I unlocked the door and lifted the bag. "Told you he's always prepared. He brought some warm clothes for you."

Rio followed me inside my apartment and took the bag when I handed it to him, though he looked a little embarrassed. "I have my own stuff."

He did. Though most of it was badly worn and in need of repair. "Now you have more stuff," I proclaimed. "How about you go wash up? I'm going to sit and read for a few minutes." I pointed at the couch, which I planned to straighten up as I'd left it a mess.

Rio seemed to debate something with himself for another minute or so. I made my way to the couch, folding up the blankets and pulling off the sheet, switching it out, and then pushing the bed back into a couch position. By the time I looked back, Rio was gone and the bathroom door was closed. I heard the shower running.

I did take a few minutes to pick up the small messes in the area. Not that there was much for clutter. Most of my things were kitchen gadgets and tools, cookbooks, and binders full of recipes. I did have subscriptions to a few cooking magazines, and a few unread, so I put everything away and sat down to wrap myself up in the chenille blanket on the couch. Didn't really think I was resting more than my body until a hand on my face startled me from sleep.

"Crap, sorry," I said, blinking and looking up at Rio. "Didn't realize I was that tired. And there's something about the winter that gets in my bones. Like I can feel the cold, so when I wrap myself up and am finally warm, it's like bam, nap time." I crawled from the little nest and folded up the blanket. My little cat nap meant I needed to get my butt down to the kitchen.

Rio was dressed, hair pulled back, thick socks on his feet, and wearing a new pair of gray sweats with a long-sleeved T-shirt. I looked him over, pleased that he didn't seem nearly as gaunt as he'd been yesterday. "I need to head back down to the kitchen to finish dinner prep. Did you want to hang out up here and rest a bit or come with?"

"I can help," Rio said. "And I'm kind of hungry."

"Well dinner is a bit of a lighter spread, but I've got lots of things I can whip up for you." He flushed again, but followed me to the door and down across to the kitchen.

Rio helped Ana and I set out the spread of food. The soup was warm and hearty, the salad divine with a homemade ranch dressing, the rolls warm, buttery, and delicate. I was so stuffed I couldn't imagine eating any of the tart or cinnamon rolls I'd made. Rio ate six rolls and half a tart. No one commented, even if they did notice. Though I knew both Zach and Sean were paying attention.

The fact that I kept offering Rio more food seemed to please them. And when I left Sean curled up with mulled cider beside the fire to make my way to kitchen cleanup, he patted my hand and murmured. "Is good."

I wasn't sure what was good. The cider? He'd had it a dozen times. But his gaze had fallen on Rio. So maybe that Rio was eating? "He's looking better, right?" I said softly. "Not so gaunt."

Sean nodded. "Keep him fed."

"That's my plan. Do you think we can convince him to stay here?"

Sean looked toward the window and the dark sky outside. "Full moon in a few days."

"Yeah? Is that a bad thing?" Did PTSD get worse during the full moon? I had thought that some old wives' tale, about the full moon making people crazy.

Sean shrugged like he wasn't sure either. But he hadn't been born and raised in America, so maybe they didn't have the same superstitions? Or perhaps they did, only some of their ideas were a bit different. I'd have to ask Zach about it later.

"I've got to clean up the kitchen," I told him as I excused myself. As soon as I began loading up the cart, Rio was by my side ready to carry the dishes. "You don't have to help," I told him. "You've worked hard today."

"You have too. Let me help."

I waved Ana away as she came to offer help as well, but I didn't need a crowded kitchen. After dinner cleanup was always the easiest of the day. It wasn't like the constant cook and prep role I worked the rest of the time. Everything was put away, the dishwasher filled, counters cleaned, and everything quietly waiting for the next morning prep to begin.

Rio and I worked in silence, him taking cues from me on what was next, and by the time I was done, I had to admit I was dragging a bit. Not enough sleep the night before. My ankle ached a little, but the walking splint helped, though I couldn't wait to sit down. I smiled up at Rio after I'd washed my hands and put the last of the cleaning supplies away. "Did you want to come back to my apartment with me, or find a place in the house?"

His breath seemed to catch, as if staring down at me and making a decision, was too much. I reached out and took his hand, squeezing it gently. "No pressure. Whatever you want."

Rio turned his hand in mine and squeezed back, his palm a pulse of warmth in mine. "Your place, if that's okay." He glanced at the house like it held some rowdy party I had yet to discover.

"Sure." I rewarded him with a smile, letting go of his hand to retrieve the supply I'd created. I had a stack of food ready for him. Stuff he could have brought to a regular room and not needed refrigeration, and if he chose my place, a couple containers in the fridge too. I piled up the stash and held out my hand again.

Rio took it, and half the containers before making his way across the kitchen with me, through the house, and to the garage. He was quiet again as we entered my place, but not a brooding sort of quiet, maybe reflective, but not in an anxious way. More at peace, perhaps? I hoped that him having plenty of food had him feeling a lot better. And I knew warmth could go a long way in curing some of the basic stress of winter life.

I dug through my drawers for more PJs. One of the perks of living in a northern climate meant that I had a stock of the warm stuff. Apparently Zach had given Rio some as well because he dug through his bags of stuff, retrieving a pair that looked like it had little bunnies on it.

"You want the bathroom first?" I asked him.

"You go ahead," Rio said.

I made my way into the bathroom to ready for the evening. Odd how tired I was. It wasn't all that late. Almost eight, though the darkness of the winter always made it feel later. I wondered if Rio would like a quiet movie night. There wasn't much else to do at my place. I brushed my teeth and opened the bathroom door to find Rio changed.

"You don't have to get ready for bed already if you don't want to," I told him. "It's pretty early."

"Do you think we'll have to go somewhere?"

"Not unless the house catches fire." I headed to the couch and began pulling it apart to make the bed out of it. "I'm thinking it's a good night for a movie and some warm blankets. No fireplace in here, sorry. But the heat works really well."

"A movie sounds great," Rio admitted. "Can't remember the last time I saw one."

"I can make you some popcorn too. The real butter kind, if you'd like. I don't have that microwave stuff, but I have an air popper which works great."

"Sure," Rio agreed. "That sounds amazing."

"No problem." I opened the chest with all the blankets and pulled them out, stacking them at the bottom of the bed, then made my way to the kitchen. "Remote is on the left side table. Power on, and the center round button will take you to a bunch of movie options."

"You don't want to choose?"

"Nah. I'm not picky. I can watch a sob fest chick flick or an action movie filled with explosions. It's all good." In the kitchen I pulled down the air popper from the top of the fridge and the largest bowl I could find. And in ten minutes I had a giant batch of fresh popcorn ready, salted and buttered.

Rio had chosen *Iron Man* and was already sitting on the couch, curled up beneath a spread of the blankets.

"Tony Stark is hot, even if he's a bit of an asshole," I remarked.

"He is," Rio agreed as I sat down beside him and handed him the bowl. "Combination of money and brains, gives him a god complex. But neither of those makes him infallible."

"You've seen this before?" I asked, digging myself into the blankets and getting close to Rio, to share his body heat. Man, he was warm. Thankfully he didn't pull away.

"When it first came out. Was recovering in a military hospital at the time."

"The beginning sort of hits home then, right?" I motioned at the screen and the opening with Stark getting caught up in a bombing and kidnapped.

"A little," Rio said. "Lots of dirt out there. At first you think you'll see anything that moves, but the landscape is all the same, so your eyes begin to glaze over all of it. And you miss stuff. Not a fan of the desert."

"The heat would be nice right now."

Rio reached over, his arm wrapping around my waist and pulling me closer. His body heat beginning to ease the lingering chill in my bones instantly. "Warm enough?"

I sighed. "Yes. Wow, you're so warm."

"One positive at least."

"Lots of things about you are good," I promised.

"You barely know me."

"Okay," I agreed. "Do you have some sordid past I should worry about? Spousal abuse? Animal torture?"

"No," Rio said, horrified.

"Then we're good."

He let out a long breath, like he was working on keeping control.

"You okay?" I hesitated. "I mean, with this. Me. Us. Close."

"Yes." He paused for a minute. "I just worry."

"About?"

"My control."

"Control? Like are you planning on jumping me? Cause I'd be on board with that."

"You don't know what you're saying. I could hurt you."

"Do you plan to?" I didn't think for a minute that he did. Had my fair share of creepy guy encounters in my life, and I did not get that vibe from him.

"No."

"We're good then."

He was quiet another minute while we watched Tony Stark become the first semblance of Iron Man. "Sorry I kissed you earlier."

"I'm okay with that. Kissing is good." His arm wrapped around me even better. I could so see myself falling asleep under his warmth, and waking up wrapped up in his embrace.

He seemed to relax a little.

"Rio," I said, "I'm good. I promise."

"And if I'm not?"

"Not good with us snuggling?"

"Not good in general."

"Again, I ask, how are you a bad guy?"

"Always hungry," he said.

"But I made you popcorn, and there is a ton of food in the kitchen for you. It's not like you're going to eat me, right?" It was a joke, the idea of him eating me, and if he hadn't looked so serious, I might have teased him about a more sexual interpretation of it, but he looked uncomfortable.

"No."

I reached over to pat his knee, leaving my hand resting there when I was done. "Then we're good. Eat. Watch the movie. Sorry if I fall asleep on you. Didn't sleep well last night."

"Sorry I kept you up."

It had been my worry for him that had kept me awake, but I wasn't going to let him take the blame. Instead I settled into his side, half using him as a heated pillow and watched the movie until sleep stole me away.

CHAPTER 13

I awoke gloriously warm, with the weight of a firm body against me. The sigh that escaped my lips sounded decadent even to me. I slowly opened my eyes to try to discern the time. My phone alarm hadn't gone off, but I couldn't recall where I'd put it.

Rio was wrapped around me, draped half across me like I was some giant teddy bear he was snuggling. And that felt grand to me. Even with his hair long and messy and the beard a bit over-grown, he smelled clean, and looked amazing with his dark lashes resting on pale cheeks.

I reached up to brush a bit of hair from his face, studying him, marveling at the little things that made him so attractive. The shape of his face, the curl of his hair, the line of his shoulder, and that delicious warmth. My personal furnace. He must have gotten up in the night sometime, as he was without the pajama top he'd come to bed in.

It was more than a little decadent to stare at all that skin. Defined lines of arms and shoulders, a strong back, none of which looked starved or gaunt. But the man had a very thick layer of dark hair dusting his skin. Not a carpet or anything so thick, but more hair than I'd ever seen on a man outside of a movie. I ran a hand over his shoulder, finding his skin warm, the hair soft, and my body instantly turned on with the idea of him all over me.

He shifted a little, breath stuttering as his eyes fluttered open, that clear blue gaze half lidded and sexy. "Morning," he whispered, eyes closing again as if unwilling to get up.

"We got a bit," I said, finding my phone on the side table. "Don't have to be awake yet. You can sleep more."

"Hmm," he said and tugged me closer. His heat making me sigh in pleasure. I could stay like this all day.

Rio tucked me beneath him, like he planned to use me as a pillow, and that was okay because I splayed my hands over his chest and the thick layer of hair there. Never thought I'd be into really hairy guys until that moment, but wow, the way it felt under my hands, and against my skin, I could imagine a lot of very not PG things that tickle could do to me.

Of course at this angle, Rio draped over me, there was really no way to hide my morning erection. And I was momentarily embarrassed. But it was a natural thing, especially waking up in bed with a hot guy. Though I couldn't stop the burn of it filling my cheeks. I was probably as red as a tomato. At least the light of the early morning wasn't bright enough to really highlight my weirdness.

"Sorry," I mumbled, looking up to meet his gaze. He seemed to be studying me, eyes focused, though still sleepy.

"For?"

"The dick digging into your thigh?" I tried.

His lips curved in the edge of a smile, while my hands still explored his chest without real thought. It was like I couldn't stop touching him. The plump tease of his nipples made me want to lick them and bite them, and I gnawed on my lip to keep from doing just that.

Rio bent down and his lips captured mine before I could

define the thousands of other things I wanted to do to him, and him to me. And that kiss devoured all the rest. I closed my eyes and sank into his embrace, wallowing in the feel of his heat, and letting him explore my mouth with his tongue. It was delicious and almost like a dream, though the throbbing of my cock said it was either a super erotic dream, or I'd find myself really in Rio's arms when I opened my eyes.

And he was still there. Blue gaze meeting mine as his long exploration of my mouth became a dance of tiny kisses. He reached down and adjusted my hips, putting my groin firmly beneath his, before adding a delightful press of his hips into mine and beginning a slow grind.

I gasped as the drag of his cock slid against mine. Even through the clothing, it was like a brand. An almost burning heat of wanton desire. "Rio," I begged, asking for everything, and not sure at all what I needed in that moment, except him.

His lips found mine again, adding a thrust of his tongue to the arching roll of our lower bodies. I clung to him, fire blazing a trail through my core, down my spine and filling my cock with need. The friction was amazing, a building of desire upon desire that had my heart racing and my breathing labored. Such a small thing.

Rio kissed a trail down the side of my face, finding my neck and even decorating my chin with soft brushes of his lips. His hips leading an unstoppable rhythm against me, the pressure racing till the edge began to become too much.

I gasped, "Gonna come."

"Mhmm," Rio hummed against my neck, his face buried against me. "Come, Montana."

I came so hard it was an eruption of blind pleasure. My fingers dug into his shoulders and his lips sucked at the skin of mine. The circling swirl of my orgasm, and the heat of pleasure poured through me, making me suck in air and struggle to find the ground again. I felt a bit like I was flying, even while Rio's fine body anchored me to the bed.

He pressed his forehead to mine, though I couldn't really see much as my vision glazed out. But he shared his breath with me, and it didn't smell like morning breath. I hoped mine didn't either, though I wasn't sure I could move yet if it did. Finally he came back into focus. His fingers traced my face, a gentle caress as he studied me.

"Wow," I whispered against his lips. "That was real, right? Not asleep having the sexiest dream ever?"

He grinned. "Keep playing with my nipples and you'll see where else this dream goes."

And I was still playing with his nipples, and his chest hair, at least with one hand. The other I'd seemed to bruise him with, my grip tight on his back. "Should I stop? I don't really want to stop… Sorry I hurt you."

"You didn't hurt me," he said. "And you don't have to stop." He reached up to grab my wrist and guide it down. He must have stripped down to just boxers in the middle of the night. They were wet, and he'd obviously come, but when Rio guided my hand beneath the fabric, I found him still hard.

"Fuck," I whispered as I wrapped my hand around him. My own cock stiffened again. His cock was like the rest of him, lean, defined, and so fucking hot I worried it would burn me. What would it feel like to have all that heat in me? Would I feel the pulse of that warmth deep inside? "Can we? Are you…? How do…?" I had so many questions that needed answers, yet all that mattered right that second was him. It wasn't smart or safe to continue without some answers, but that didn't stop my body from screaming for more. I slid my hand up and down his length, grip tight around him, like I wanted to be in that moment.

Rio kissed my face, dancing around my lips before finding them for a moment and retracing my tongue with his. He pulled out of the kiss and looked me in the eyes, one hand on my face, half curled in my hair. Had I noticed before that he had such large hands? I wanted all of that, all of him wrapped around me. But his stomach growled, a loud gurgling thing that surprised me with its intensity and then my phone alarm went off.

"Fuck," I growled. "Wanna stay in bed with you." My hand wrapped around him felt like it needed to stay there. But he was hungry, and my instinct was to feed him. "I need to get up."

Rio shoved the blankets back, pulling himself free from my grasp for a moment. Instantly I felt the loss of his heat, but he didn't run away. Instead he tugged my pajama bottoms down, freeing my cock from the fabric and making me shiver at the come cooling around me, even as my dick throbbed in need for him again.

"Rio?"

He bent and took me in his mouth. Heat engulfing the length of me, almost too hot, suction instantly making me breathless. There was no stopping it. And I would look back later with a bit of embarrassment at how fast I came again, pouring myself into his mouth. He swallowed every drop of my spend even as I gasped and writhed beneath him, begging him for more in unintelligible words. I felt boneless, nerves awake, alive, and as limp as overcooked spaghetti. He pulled my pajamas back up, then reached up to caress my face again.

"You?" I gasped out, wanting to return the favor, but not sure I could get my body to move yet.

"Another time," he said, his gaze intense.

I blinked at him, brain stuttering with my body's slow return to normal. My heart began to come down, and my shoulder oddly throbbed. Had he bitten me? It didn't feel like it. Not exactly, but the thought of him biting me would have made me hard again if I'd been able. Instead I stared at him, half in awe, and half just stunned. The fact that he didn't jump right out of bed to get on with the day gave me hope. Would he stay? Was he interested in me? Or was I just convenient?

In reality, I barely knew him. It was unfair to feel so drawn to him and not know. Was I throwing myself at him? I sort of did that a lot in my life.

He breathed out a long breath and frowned. "Suddenly so serious."

"Sorry. I'm just overthinking. Bad habit." My alarm went off again, set on a cycle to keep me from falling back to sleep. I had to get moving. I struggled to sit up, and Rio moved, helping me find a bit of balance even while I missed his warmth.

He traced his fingers over my neck, frown deepening. "Sorry. Didn't mean to mark you."

I reached up to feel the spot where my shoulder met my neck. I didn't feel anything, no punctures or anything, though the skin was a bit tender. A hickey perhaps? I'd check when I got to the bathroom. "Not hurt, but I do need to get ready for the day."

He stared at me a moment longer, close enough that I could reach out and pull him in for a kiss. So, I did. I expected him to pull away. He didn't. Rio accepted my kiss and stayed in my space a bit longer, like he was reluctant for the moment to end too.

"Don't let this get weird," I told him. "I like you. That's okay, yeah?"

"It's not safe," he said softly. "I shouldn't have…" he glanced away.

I touched his face, forcing him to look back at me. "Consenting adult here."

"I could have hurt you." His gaze fell back to my shoulder.

"You didn't break the skin. Not that I can tell."

"No," he agreed.

I shrugged. "I'm good then."

His stomach growled again, sounding a bit like a monster clawing its way free from the darkness. I gaped at him.

"Guess I need to feed you, yeah?"

"I need to eat," he agreed.

"Good. Food is my forte."

Rio's smile was enough to ease some of my tension and get me moving. I had a man to feed.

CHAPTER 14

B reakfast was fast, and I badly needed to restock the kitchen with fresh things like veggies and fruits. Zach didn't arrive until the tail end of the meal, appearing in the kitchen as we were cleaning up instead of the dining room.

"Are the roads clear?" I asked.

"As far as I can tell, yes. Looks like another storm is headed in our direction. Tomorrow or the day after," Zach told me as he filled his plate with eggs and leftover bacon. There was already a tray set aside for Sean who had a more traditional Asian breakfast. Though since he still sort of ate like a bird, it was mostly tea and some soup.

"I need to get to the grocery store." With the way Rio ate I might just need an increase in the food budget. Would Zach get mad if I brought that up? He'd never questioned it before, and Mr. Yamamoto paid most of the bills. But a major increase might raise flags, especially since there were no events planned in the near future.

Zach's gaze flicked to Rio. "Yeah, with another mouth to feed, restocking is a good idea."

Rio frowned and looked away. "I don't want to be a burden."

"You're not," I promised him, tugging at the collar of my sweater a bit. Without Rio's warmth I'd been chilly, and since he'd left me a very glaring hickey, I'd chosen to wear a sweater with a draping turtleneck sort of thing. I'd need to see if one of the staff knew a way to make it less scratchy in the wash because it was driving me nuts.

"I make sure all my people are fed," Zach said looking between us. Could he tell we'd sort of done a thing? "Let me know once you've cleaned up and I'll drive you down. Don't want to chance your car getting stuck."

"I can't fit that much in my car anyway," I agreed. Meanwhile, I could really load up his truck. "Can we stop at the food bank so I can drop off bread?"

"Of course," Zach agreed.

That had me moving faster, zipping through the cleanup and bagging up the bread. Some supplies we got delivered in bulk, like flour and sugar, but other things I preferred to choose for myself. And my shopping list was full of fruits and fresh veggies, things I was certain Rio hadn't had in a while.

"I'll wait here," Rio whispered.

"You don't want to come?"

He seemed hesitant.

"There won't be a lot of people. There never is in the middle of the week," I assured him. But his grip on the counter didn't loosen. I wondered if his illness, whatever it was that made him hungry all the time, would make him more vulnerable to the virus. That thought made me want to keep him home where he was safe. "You don't have to go. You can go back to my place and rest if you want."

"If you'll check the fireplaces while we're gone," Zach said to Rio, "that would be great. Make sure everyone is stocked with firewood. You know where the wood is."

"I can do that," Rio agreed.

I stared at him a moment longer. I patted his hand. "There are containers of snacks in the fridge for you. Anything you've been craving?"

A hint of a smile curved his lips as he looked at me, like maybe it was me he wanted. And that little idea made warmth curl through my stomach. I wanted to throw myself at him. Not exactly a good idea in front of the boss. Instead he said, "Those cinnamon rolls were amazing. Ever made the sticky bun kind? With the nuts on them? Haven't had those since I was a kid."

"I'm on board with that," Zach agreed and patted his stomach, "Though I don't need the sugar. Can't recall ever having a sticky bun that wasn't store bought."

I gaped at him. "What? Then you've never had a sticky bun. Real sugar, honey, and butter? How have you lived this long?"

"Deprived apparently." He pointed at my phone. "Add it to your list and grab your jacket. It's still an icebox out there." He headed toward the garage. "We'll be back before lunch," he told Rio. "Sean might have things to do to keep you busy."

"I'll help as best I can," Rio agreed.

I smiled, hoping that he was finding a place here at the manor and would stay. I could work with him not wanting to leave much. Other than my weekly shopping trip to refill the pantry, I hadn't left much either since the pandemic started. It was just safer to stay home. The few friends I had were more than willing to Facetime or ramble on a call with me while I cooked. I sent them cookies for the holidays and they sent me daily memes to keep me laughing. Life had been more isolated in the last year, but not all that different from the previous one, partly living this far north and working in a very small area. I did plan that once this pandemic finally ended, I'd have my friends up for a week-end. Perhaps I'd even get them signed up for some classes, show them how to make moon cakes or mochi ice cream.

I triple checked my list before getting in Zach's waiting truck, bundled up like I was ready for a trek into the tundra rather than a heated car to a heated grocery store. He'd put the lid on the truck bed, to protect the inside from the snow and ice, but it also meant I had plenty of room to fill the truck with supplies.

"Rio eats a lot," I told him as we headed toward town.

The roads were better, though still icy. And so few cars were out that the black ice at the stop signs and lights was almost inevitable. Zach powered through it all, his attention focused on the road.

"It's fine," Zach said. "Buy what you need."

"It will increase the budget," I said quietly.

"It's okay," Zach said. "I'd rather have him fed than out there hungry."

Our first stop was the food bank. I donned my mask, even wrapping the scarf around my face as an added layer to keep out the cold, before jumping out to help Zach unload the bread. Diana and Jim were there to help carry it inside.

"Anything low on stock?" Zach asked them. "I can order from the grocery store, have them deliver."

"Canned goods are always necessary. Been hard to get right now as there's a new rush of panic shopping," Diana admitted. "Whatever you can provide would be appreciated."

Zach nodded. "I'll have stuff sent over. Whatever we can get a hold of." He got the last of the bread unloaded and we headed back to the truck. I was already worrying over my list. I didn't often use canned ingredients, not when fresh was so much better, but what if shelves were empty again?

"We'll be fine," Zach assured me as we pulled up to the small grocery store. It was all we had in town. "I'll drive down to the city tomorrow if I have to."

I shouldn't have been food anxious. We had a good supply at the house. Enough for a few weeks at least. And I could be very inventive with the menu. But we had to feed Rio now too, and I worried he'd go hungry just to ensure we all ate.

The grocery was mostly empty and I grabbed a cart. If I had to can veggies myself, I would. And right then I planned to make a stock of homemade soups, canned and ready to warm, enough to get us through a couple weeks of this bitter cold at least. Zach did not try to hurry me through produce or beyond. Since the store was mostly empty, he went in search of the manager to get an order sent over to the food bank.

By the time we were headed back, it was almost lunchtime. I hoped Ana had jumped on lunch prep, but if not, I could throw together a sandwich bar in minutes. When we pulled up to the house, closest to the kitchen door, Rio appeared, heading our way in little more than a pair of boots and light sweater. He had found the wagon I often used to drag supplies in, and towed it to the back of the truck to unload.

Once inside I was roasting, too much lifting and moving with the temperature change. I stood in the mudroom and stripped out of the winter gear, even tugging off the sweater to leave just the white undershirt before stepping into my house slippers. A pot bubbled on the stove and Ana greeted us with a smile. She'd started the soup for lunch, which meant I had to make the toasted sandwiches yet, but that was easy enough.

Sean appeared in the doorway, his long hair pulled back, and his gaze searching for his lover. He glanced at me, found Zach and smiled, then looked back at me, his smile falling away.

What? I looked behind me, wondering if something was wrong. But there was no one there since Zach and Rio were loading supplies onto the counter.

"He bit you?" Sean asked in alarm.

Oh. I felt heat flush up my cheeks. The shirt collar apparently revealed the edge of the hickey. "No broken skin. I'll cover it while I cook," I said, wondering if he had some weird hang-up about physical marks.

Zach appeared by my side, tugging at the collar to examine it. He glared at Rio.

"I'm fine," I promised, feeling like I wanted to sink into the floor and vanish. "I'm a consenting adult, you know."

Rio looked away.

"How bad of a bite does it have to be?" Zach asked Sean.

"It's a blood curse. More than broken skin," Rio interrupted. "Would have to be a pretty bad bite. Not life threatening exactly, but bleeding intensely. He's fine. It was an accident. It won't happen again."

I blinked at them all, feeling a bit like they were speaking a different language. "I'm standing right here. It's not like he'd rip me up, and I'd just let him."

"The full moon is in two days," Sean said softly, looking at Zach instead of Rio.

"I can already feel it," Rio agreed. "I should go…"

I reached out and grabbed his arm. "No way. There's a storm coming. You heard Zach earlier. You have no place to go."

His eyes met mine and they were sad. "I don't want to hurt you."

"I'm not hurt."

"This time."

I wanted to scream, but instead I threw my arms around his middle, not caring if Zach saw and thought it was unprofessional. "You can't go out there. It's not safe."

"I'm not safe."

"I don't understand."

"I'm hungry," Rio said. "Always hungry."

"Then let me feed you." I tugged away from him to dig out sandwich fixings. "We bought plenty."

But Rio's gaze was on the floor instead of on me.

"Stay," Zach said after a moment, making my heart flip over with hope. "It's not safe for you out there. As long as we keep you fed, you'll be safe."

"Maybe," Rio said quietly. "I never stay around others…"

"We'll work it out. Just let us know if you need some space. If it gets to be too much."

Rio still looked undecided, but he wrapped his arms around

me, his face resting in my hair, seeming to breathe in the scent of me.

"It's okay," I said, not even sure of what was wrong. "I trust you."

"I don't trust me," he said quietly.

I trusted him enough for the both of us. "Let me get you some food." I tugged out of his embrace, missing his warmth immediately, but got to work on the meal. Food I could do. It was easy, predictable, and I had the answers to pretty much any possibility of issues that came up in the kitchen. It was Rio that I found confusing. Frustrating even. There was something they weren't telling me. But I had plans to ask lots of questions, see if I could discern an answer even without asking them outright, which I didn't think would help. I just hoped it didn't make Rio want to run away.

CHAPTER 15

The day passed fast. Rio moved about, keeping busy with random house chores and an occasional trip to help me in the kitchen. I kept a snack plate out for him, so if he got hungry, he could stop in, grab some food and go back to whatever he was working on.

I created a massive batch of sticky buns, and dinner was steak, baked potatoes, and broccoli. Zach had sent me a text to up the protein and red meat over the next few days, which had me scrambling to unthaw things.

As I was searing the steaks Rio wrapped his arms around me from behind, and I couldn't help but smile. "Hi," I said.

"That smells amazing."

"Medium, okay? Zach likes lots of pink in his, so do most of the rest of his staff, and Sean has fish for dinner," I pointed to the skillet I'd already set aside to keep warm.

"Medium is great. Enough to take the chill off is all I really need."

I was tempted to launch into a lecture about cooking temps and the destruction of bacteria through heat, but it was one of those moments I decided to keep the science to myself. I set the tongs down and turned in his arms. A few days of eating and he seemed so much healthier. Instead of gaunt and tired, he had filled out, like he'd put on muscle, though I knew that was impossible in such a short time. But he looked healthy and well rested.

"You look good. Better. You feel okay?"

"Hungry, but good," Rio agreed. He paused and stared out the window at the darkness. Then he said, "I don't sleep well during the full moon."

"I've heard it can really bother some people. Maybe I can help somehow?"

"Yeah? How would that work?"

"I can make you sleepy time tea," I offered as I reached up to touch his face, tracing the lines of his cheek and strong jaw. Rio was a very handsome man. "Or wear you out in other ways."

A smile tugged at the corner of his lips. "These other ways of yours sound nefarious."

"They could be, or angelic. I'm flexible," I said arching up on my tiptoes to reach his lips and kiss him. He accepted, returning the kiss, but breaking it off to point at the stove. I flipped the steak, able to tell by the browning and smell where we were at.

"Might be better to wait a few days," Rio said sounding a bit sad.

"Wait? For sleep you mean? Or other activities?" Did he think we were moving too fast? I supposed we kind of were, but my relationships had sort of been that way. A quick flare of attraction, though often the other guy got bored with me. I spent too much time cooking or talking about food. At least Rio enjoyed my cooking and didn't whine about how a pizza would be better. He ate whatever I made.

Rio kissed my cheek. "Patience is good."

"Can we talk about the curse?" I asked, wondering if he would give me details. The way he, Zach and Sean talked about it, it sounded like a real curse. I thought perhaps it was a medical thing. But in my few breaks during the day, searching on my phone, I couldn't find anything that seemed to account for what I'd experienced. And nothing that made him this hungry was contagious. "Do you have some kind of tapeworm or something?"

He let out a long sigh. "No."

I pulled one of the steaks from the pan and added the next. "You can't talk about it?"

"Just know that you can't catch what I have. Not unless our blood mingles."

"I'm not really into blood play," I said trying to think of the handful of times I'd been a bit kinky in the bedroom. The bite had been on the edge of that line. I wasn't into pain. Had dated a guy for a few months that had been into spanking, but even that was not my thing. "I'm pretty vanilla," I said. "Sorry if that's boring. Food play is about as kinky as I get. Some whipped cream, or caramel sauce, I'd be into that…"

Rio laughed lightly. "Nothing to be sorry for, other than the idea of you covered in caramel just made me hard."

I grinned up at him. "Then we're on the same page."

He sobered again, looking sad. "Sometimes my control sucks."

"Have you ever hurt anyone?"

"Not on purpose."

I thought about that for a minute. "A lover?"

"No. It was when I left the military. Right after I was changed…"

"If it has been a long time, maybe your control is better?"

"Haven't been around people much to test it. Better safe than sorry."

"Does the full moon make you grumpy? Moody? I have a friend whose dogs get all weird and howl. Every month like clockwork. Full moon and they sing the song of their people."

"Song of their people?" Rio seemed amused. "Sounds annoying for their owner."

"Dog dad," I corrected. Because Brand treated those dogs like his kids. "He doesn't mind. He has a good size plot of land so they can run around and be dogs. They seem happy."

"Just to howl at the moon?"

I shrugged. "It doesn't always have to be big things. I'm happy to be cooking for people. Sometimes it's not the big things so much as a culmination of little things, yeah?"

He stared at me for a minute or so, his gaze intense, but less guarded. "Yeah."

"Let's not worry so much about what's to come. I'll keep you fed. And all will be okay."

He pulled me into his arms again, squeezing me almost tight enough to hurt, then said, "I hope you're right."

"I'm always right. It's part of being young and fabulous."

Now he did laugh. "Okay, I'll agree to that."

I patted his chest. "Get the cart ready, dinner is about to be served."

"Can't wait for steak, but those sticky buns have been tempting me all afternoon."

"I made lots for you," I said.

"I'll take your sticky buns any day, over all the rest."

I felt my cheeks heat with embarrassment. Had he meant that to sound sexual? And of course, my body responded. I so needed looser pants. I shooed him away to work on building the warming trays. Food first, then I'd drag him off for a bit of making out on my couch.

Dinner was good and everyone moaned over the sticky buns, wondering why I hadn't made them sooner. I promised to add them to the semi-regular rotation. By the time I dragged Rio upstairs, both of us bogged down with food, I ached to curl up with him, to taste his lips sweetened by the honey and nuts. Rio, however, was being overly cautious. Kisses he allowed, but that was it.

Wrapped up in his arms, aching for him, I wanted him to throw a bit of caution to the wind.

"In a couple of days," Rio promised.

"Is this the full moon thing again? Are you a werewolf or something?" I teased. "Sexy times make you wolf out?"

"Not sexy times," Rio said softly. He reached up and captured my hand, delivering a kiss to my palm. Then he rolled me into the heat of his embrace, wrapping himself around me, which made me both hard as a rock and sleepy at the same time. "It's not really like the romance novels. Sexy alphas in control, demanding the submission of their omega."

I laughed. "You read omegaverse? Next you'll tell me you love mpreg."

"I've read mpreg," Rio agreed. Then he let out a long sigh. "Haven't read in a while."

Then I remembered his place had been destroyed by the snow. He probably hadn't had a lot of money for books prior to that. Though I'd made sure the local library had a fair share of gay romance with my special requests. "I have lots you can borrow."

"For pointers?" he teased.

"Sure," I agreed.

"Sounds good to me," Rio agreed.

I sighed, but let it go. No reason to push. We had time, I hoped. Keeping Rio busy at the manor seemed to give him purpose, which had him talking about leaving less. And that had become my new goal. Keep him busy, mind focused on tasks rather than his internal struggles. With him fed and warm, he was finding a groove with the rest of us, and that made me happy, even if he wouldn't end up with me in the long-term.

I tried not to think about that. The idea that once he was healthy and stable, he might not want to stay. Was I just convenient to him? A willing body? The thought made me a bit melancholy. I dozed a bit; I couldn't seem to drop off into actual deep sleep. Lying beside him for a while I tried to focus on recipes instead of my internal frustrations. And it was almost midnight when Rio seemed to either fall into a fitful sleep, or check into a nightmare that grabbed his heart and squeezed because he made some very whining dog-like sounds, and writhed in his sleep. Was this the moon thing he'd worried about? Another strange checked box in the list of oddities he seemed to have?

I turned his way, shaking him gently, trying to break the grip of the dream. No response. I shook him a bit harder, finally having to dig my fingers into his shoulders a little to even get a hold.

He snarled and turned swiftly, pinning me to the bed, teeth bared. My heart flipped over in a moment of fear, the first I'd had since I'd met him. A sinking feeling rolled through me, terror that he'd hurt me, and sadness that I'd misread him. Only he'd warned me, hadn't he? Said the full moon made him restless. And I'd been reading up on PTSD. Which meant his reaction could be completely based on what he was seeing, which might not have been me at all, but rather some war zone he'd survived.

I relaxed in his arms, letting him go and not offering any aggression or fast movement at all. Instead I gently touched his cheek, keeping my caress light, focused on slowing my racing heart and banishing blame that had no use to either of us.

"Rio," I called softly. "Baby, come back to me. You can hear me, right? Feel my caress? I'd never hurt you." I whispered over and over, while he seemed to struggle with himself. His grip hurt, the weight of him holding me down more than a little scary, but he also seemed half frozen. Face contorted, still in a partial snarl, though it began to ease as he seemed to finally sense my touch.

The steam went out of him all at once and he frowned down at me. He reached over and turned the light on, making me blink away spots. "Did I hurt you?" He demanded.

"Just a little bruised. I'm fine," I assured him.

He stared at me, the spots where he'd grabbed me reddened and throbbing a bit with the coming bruises.

"I'm fine," I repeated, resting my palm on his face. "You were having a nightmare. Do you want to talk about it?"

Slowly he uncurled his hands from me and backed away making my heart flip over. He got out of bed and headed to the kitchen. "I should eat."

I crawled out of bed too. "Okay. Let me make you something."

Rio shook his head. "You go to sleep. There's plenty I can manage on my own."

"Maybe some sleepy time tea will help?" I offered. He paced the kitchen, pulling things out of the fridge, but still looking more agitated, more like a cornered animal than anything I'd ever seen from him. Perhaps it was lingering anxiety from the nightmare? Brand was a psychologist, maybe he'd be able to give me some specific answers about how to help Rio. I planned to call him in the morning.

Rio crossed the kitchen to stand in front of me. He gave me a light kiss on the lips. "Go rest. No need for both of us to be awake all night. I promise I'll keep the noise down."

I stared into those clear eyes and wondered how I could help. "Rio?"

"It's okay," he said. "This is normal for me."

Normal was his heart rate being up? I could feel it pulsing through his skin. His pupils were also dilated, leaving very little of that beautiful blue left. His movements, agitated and jittery, made it almost seem like he was uncomfortable in his own skin.

"Rio," I whispered, feeling helpless.

"Let me eat. You rest. Please," he begged.

I breathed out a long breath, counting slowly so as to not create my own panic, but nodded. "Okay. You'll wake me if you need something?"

"Yes," he said. He turned the small light near the stove on, then turned off the rest of the lights. "Sleep."

I crawled back into bed; certain I wasn't going to be able to sleep.

Not with worrying about him. The blankets were still warm, and the pillows smelled like him. I watched him move around the kitchen for a while, opening containers, eating ten times the amount of food I thought most people could. It became a bit hypnotic, and I didn't realize I'd closed my eyes until long after I'd fallen asleep and was suddenly jolted awake by the alarm on my phone.

Most of the time I slept well enough that I woke before the alarm, usually rested and ready to confront the day. Today I just felt tired and the alarm was like a bomb warning flashing through my skull.

I was cold, which never boded well in the morning, and even more so as I wondered if Rio had not come to bed. When I sat up and turned on the light, a sick feeling flipped over in my gut. The empty bed and kitchen, just two small indicators. The bag of supplies and clothing, which had been sitting beside the bathroom door, missing, was the next dagger in my heart. The bathroom door was open, so I knew he wasn't in there. And my place didn't really have any hidden nooks or crannies he could vanish into.

Had he gone to the main house maybe? Worried that he'd wake me, maybe I'd find him in the kitchen over there. Or even up and helping Zach already. I hurried through my morning routine and rushed over to the manor, the last threads of hope stretching thin.

The kitchen was empty, untouched as it was most mornings when I arrived. The entire house was still, no one really awake yet, and if Zach had tucked Rio away in an unused room, I couldn't find any indication of him.

As I made coffee, nausea and anxiety began to swirl through me. He wouldn't have left *left* would he? Like gone back to his place? It wasn't livable and there was a storm coming. When I checked the weather app on my phone it said the storm would arrive in the late afternoon and continue for at least another twenty-four hours. The snow and following temperature drop all too familiar with this year's brutal weather patterns.

I was halfway through breakfast, fresh croissants resting on the counter when I couldn't take the anxiety anymore and sent Zach a text. Maybe he would give me good news. Maybe Rio was fast asleep in some room in the house, and I just didn't know it yet. I prepped the meal as though he were there and would need the food.

Zach arrived in the kitchen looking somber. My heart rolled over in my chest and I gripped the counter.

"The sled is gone. Did he take any food?" Zach asked.

I peered around the kitchen trying to think through my supplies, but if something had been missing, it wasn't from here. And I'd barely glanced through the stock in my tiny kitchen. "I don't know?" I reached out for Zach, terrified now. "There's another storm coming. He can't be out there in this."

Zach took a hold of my hands and squeezed them. "Breathe, Montana. It will be okay."

"But he's out there, with nowhere to go and no food. With a storm coming."

"He's not stupid. He'll come back."

I shook my head thinking of the nightmare I'd woken him from. He'd been so afraid he'd hurt me. Had that driven him away? "It's all my fault."

"It's not," Zach said. He let me go and patted my back. "Focus on the food. I'll keep an eye out for Rio. I think we just need to be patient."

"He had a nightmare last night," I confessed. "I tried to wake him…"

"Did he hurt you?" Zach asked, looking concerned. Why was everyone so certain Rio would hurt me?

"No. Of course he didn't. It was a PTSD thing. Hard to wake him completely. I'm fine. Though I think it freaked him out a little." I tried not to be annoyed with my boss. I'd never had a boss who cared at all before, and Zach sort of obsessed over the health and welfare of his employees.

Zach nodded. "Okay. I'll keep an eye out for him. It's probably just a stress response."

"What if he doesn't come back before the storm?"

"I'll check at his place, see if he's been back there."

"Thank you," I said, a little relieved, though certain that Rio wouldn't return to the trailer. "Maybe we can track the sled?"

"I did. But once I hit the trees, the ice must have made it slide because the tracks vanished." He let out a long sigh. "I'm sorry, Montana. I wish there was more I could do. Let me make sure the house is prepped for the storm, then I'll run over to his place and see if he's there."

"I understand." Even if it didn't stop me from being both heartbroken and terrified for him. "He left to keep me safe."

"Probably," Zach agreed.

"Maybe you can tell me why he's so worried?" I prodded.

"It's complicated." He stared at me for a minute. "Not sure you'd believe it anyway."

"I'm not sure what I believe anymore. He acts like he's really cursed. But while PTSD is bad, it's not a curse. Just an illness."

"I think the PTSD is only part of the problem," Zach said. "Maybe think of it as a curse? Something therapy and medicine can't control. Something that will never go away, but needs to be managed."

"But curses can be broken," I pointed out. "At least it's that way in the books."

"Not all curses can be broken."

"Then I can help him manage it."

"Once we get him back, sure." Zach headed for the mudroom to tug on all his cold gear. "It's the curse that makes him hungry. The hunger can make him dangerous, uncontrollable."

"You all act like he's going to become some raging beast," I protested.

"It might be better if you think of him that way. Hungry equals danger."

"I've been feeding him," I said softly, wondering if I should have done more.

"And he was managing well."

"But he still left."

"We'll work on that." Zach, clad in all his gear, headed for the door. "Keep the coffee going, and food on the warmer."

I nodded, though I would have done that anyway. All I could do was pray that Zach found Rio before the storm got too terrible. And I kept replaying last night in my mind. His nightmare, the awakening, and his agitation. How did I fix any of that?

CHAPTER 16

Making massive amounts of food didn't help my anxiety, but it kept me occupied. The snow began to fall after lunch, another batch of giant fluffy flakes, and I wanted to scream. No sign of Rio. Zach's texts had been odd.

Only tracks near the trailer are wolf, Zach had sent me.

Did that mean wolves had taken over his trailer? I worried since Rio hadn't been back, that he'd be stuck in some frozen hollow somewhere. *Like a pack of them?* I sent back, worried Rio would be overwhelmed or attacked if he did go home.

Just one. The three-dot note appeared for a while as though Zach were typing some long message, but finally all that appeared was, *He'll be fine.*

Rio? Or the wolf?

Will Rio go back to his trailer? I sent back.

Maybe? Zach sent back. *It is his land, and there are bears to the north of the manor, so he's unlikely to head that way.*

My heart leapt into my throat. Bears? *You found bear tracks?*

Yes. A while back, after first snow, pretty far north, but they still come looking for food.

Don't bears hibernate?

115

Yes and no. Zach sent. *It's a bit more complicated than the child-hood cartoons lead us to believe. Let's just hope Rio stays south.*

As if I didn't have enough anxiety. Now I had to worry about Rio meeting bears. And a wolf was stalking his place. Could he use the place at all? Maybe if he cleared some of the roof and propped up a bit of it around the fireplace. I hadn't seen the inside after the collapse, not like Zach had.

I focused on making canned soups, so if anyone needed something separate from a regular shared meal, they had options. I also baked bread and sticky buns until I worried I'd run out of flour. Dinner was ready to go, something more elaborate than I'd originally planned, but Ana was taking over for me. She wrung her hands as I packed up supplies.

"Wait for Zach," she said. "It's still snowing."

"I'm just going to drop food at Rio's house. I won't even leave the car until the snow stops," I said. As soon as the snow stopped the cold would drop. Which meant I had to get there fast. I filled every thermos I could find with hot cocoa, coffee, and tea. The food was another story. I had a half dozen loaves of bread, four pounds of bacon, two dozen hard boiled eggs, deviled as Rio really seemed to like those, a jumbo broccoli salad, and an entire pan of sticky buns, ready to go.

"Then wait for Zach and go tomorrow."

"It's fine," I said. Zach had texted to say he'd be late to dinner. He'd gone down to the city after checking at Rio's place, to order groceries sent up from one of the bigger chains. He wouldn't be back until late, and it was already growing dark. "Just make sure dinner is on the table."

Ana stared at me with worry as I loaded up the wagon and began dragging things out to my car. I folded the back seat down and loaded in everything, filling it up like a Tetris puzzle. I even found a tent tucked away in the side of the garage, and a portable propane grill with what appeared to be a couple of full canisters. There was also a can of bear spray, which when I read the back of, sounded like a really good idea, so I added that to the pile too.

I really hoped the new snow tires helped on the roads because when I backed the car out of the garage, the driveway was a slippery mess of growing snow piles. At least the temperatures were warm enough that it wasn't freezing to solid ice right away.

As I drove toward Rio's house, I gripped the steering wheel, white knuckled as the car slipped a little, right and left, even though I kept my speed down. It was terrifying, like driving on an ice rink, not that I'd ever done that either. I could hear the tires crunching through the snow, feel them help the car from spinning out or completely sliding off the road. And it took more than an hour to get the handful of miles to Rio's.

The little off-road section appeared to have been plowed quickly, a haphazard shove of the snow toward the trees. Probably Zach's work with the plow on his truck rather than anything the state might have done. The path hadn't been cleared, but I pulled off into the parking area hoping I wouldn't get stuck. I bundled up and pulled out the shovel Zach had left me. I didn't plan to shovel the entire walk to Rio's place, but use it more like a plow, pushing show aside to let me walk more freely. I was thankful the splint for my ankle fit under my Ugg boots as I hoped to keep my feet as warm and dry as possible.

Shoveling was exhausting. Even if I was just letting the snow fall to the edges of a narrow path. There appeared to be a dozen or so crossings of the wolf tracks. I didn't know enough about them to determine if they were from multiple wolves or just one. On TV wolves were always shown to survive in packs. I knew the perpetuated culture of "alpha males" in wolves had been disproven, and they were a more social society, protecting the weak and elders, the pack led by more of a council of females than one young brash male. It made sense really, certainly more sense than one super strong male somehow having the knowledge and willpower to take care of an entire pack by himself, but it made me wonder about lone wolves too. What did a lone wolf do without a pack? How did it survive? Wolves were pack animals by nature, needing their community to build a solid structure and even to hunt most of the time. Did that mean if this was a lone wolf, it was out there hungry and alone?

I shivered, the chill settling in more at the thought of being attacked by a wolf than the cold. The narrow path I'd dug made it easy to get to the trailer. And the path didn't feel so long now that the snow had already faded. Though I could tell the cold was settling in.

I dug the wagon out of the car, thankful it was one of those little fold up kinds with sides that popped up. It took three trips to get everything to the trailer. I tugged at the trailer door, pulling it open. I couldn't see anything inside, not even with a flashlight. I set up a little area beside the trailer, cleared away some of the snow to create a ring, and built a fire once again thanking the survival classes I'd taken at the manor.

The fire melted the snow near it, and I set up a tarp a few feet away to unload all the supplies and build the tent around it. Hopefully the fire would keep the wolf away. I put together the tent, though it was smaller than I had hoped. The windows zipped shut against the wind, and the door seemed much the same. It was pretty high end from what I could tell, and when I pulled out a box of blankets and those thermal foil looking things, I hoped it would be enough. The idea was that if Rio showed up, he'd have not only the fire for warmth, but the tent filled with blankets for a windbreak.

The fire burned pretty steady. The wood Rio had around his house a bit wet on top, but once I chiseled that first piece out, the rest seemed fine, so I added logs to keep it going, and to create a little seating area outside the tent. The heat was delightful, and since I was tired and a little sweaty, I kept close to it, hoping that Rio would see the smoke and come home.

The wind settled, for which I breathed a sigh of relief. I'd only gotten the tent stakes so far into the ground, so I kept worrying that the wind would grab it, and fling it. I'd stacked the food inside to try to keep it down. The towering trees helped as a windbreak, but I could hear the howl of it pick up every once in a while. When it fell completely still, I relaxed a little. The darkness was unnerving. Even with the fire in front of me and the frozen trailer behind me, I worried something was out there. Even felt a bit like I was being watched.

I focused on how I was feeling physically. Cold? Numb? Not really. Close to the fire I was warm and my tummy rumbled with hunger. Since I was camping in the cold, I decided to make a normal camping thing. That meant hot dogs on a stick. I dug out a pack and found the metal sticks that had been tucked away in the garage near the propane stove.

The first hot dog I burned. Hmm. Some chef I was. Burning hot dogs. The second took a long time because I worried it would burn. But I ate it finally, finding it cold in the middle. At least they were precooked so I didn't have to worry about bacteria.

"Instead you'll just freeze to death, if you don't die of starvation from burning hot dogs," I snarked at myself. Two more hot dogs and I think I had it down. They were kind of plain on their own. "Should have brought uncooked bacon, wrapped them up and cooked them that way." I was trying to save all the other supplies for Rio.

When I checked my phone it was late, almost nine, and I had no service, so even if Zach had texted me, I wouldn't get it until I was back in range. Ana would tell him where I went, and that was okay. If something happened to me, he'd know where to look.

The cold really began to drop. The snow around seemed to crystallize with that sort of glass breaking sound. If not for the crackling of the fire, I'd have been in complete silence simply listening to the cold devour everything.

I sat on a section of cut logs, curled in on myself, burrowed in the warmth of my coat, gloves, hat, and a borrowed pair of snow pants. At first it seemed okay. The fire kept me warm, and without the wind, the cold was manageable. But the chill began to seep through as exhaustion killed my adrenaline. I admit I had sort of hoped Rio had been close and would randomly pop up right away. I'd convince him to come back to the manor with me and all would be well. Though the tent and mass of supplies I'd brought meant it seemed more realistic that he would remain here. This was his land, his home, and he felt safe here. Even without a solid four walls.

How long should I stay? Was he out there maybe watching? Worried that if he came back before I left that he'd be convinced to return to the manor? I thought about heading back to the car. Didn't know if it would even make it back through the snowy roads. I had thought I'd get stuck several times on the slow trek up even with the fancy new tires.

But I sat in the dark, cooking up hot dogs and putting them on a plate nibbling one, but cooking the rest just in case. Rio had to be hungry. Maybe the smell would draw him in? All I could do was hope, even while sleepiness tugged at me and I wished for a place on my couch, curled up in blankets and sipping mulled cider.

I didn't realize I dozed until a wicked growl woke me. I jolted upward, half falling off my log seat and scrambling to keep from landing in the fire. A wolf stood on the other side of the fire, muzzle buried in the plate of cooked hot dogs, slurping, growling and occasionally glancing up at me like it expected me to take them away.

I worked really hard not to move or scream, though my lungs felt tight with the terror in my chest. The animal was huge, light gray in color, white in front with an ombre gray effect rolling over his coat, and eerily familiar clear blue eyes. The light of the fire danced across its coat, outlining the muscular form and long legs. Were wolves normally that large? I tried to recall the few times I'd seen them in zoos in my life, but they'd always been farther away, so it was hard to tell.

What was the mantra Steve Irwin and all those nature buffs used to say? The animal was more scared of us than we were of them? I wasn't sure I believed that right then with the size of the wolf's teeth.

The wolf finished the hot dogs and licked the plate before looking up and staring at me. My breath caught, afraid for a minute it was going to decide I was its next meal. But it turned toward the tent, nosing into it where all the food was stored. I guess it had been good I'd left the door mostly unzipped so it hadn't been necessary for it to tear through the fabric. The claws of the wolf were huge, dragging out bags and tearing into loaves of bread, even finding the sticky buns, which it devoured. I wasn't sure that was good for a wolf, but wasn't about to try to lecture it on wellness issues.

In fact, I sat frozen, worried that it was going through all the food I'd brought for Rio, but also a bit resigned. What did a wolf eat out here all alone in a blizzard? Were any rabbits or other prey animals out in the snow? Somehow, I felt like the pickings were pretty scarce right now. It couldn't eat everything, could it?

Since the wolf was rummaging around the tent, I turned to the bag I'd set beside me and dug out a moon cake. Had a dozen with me, since other than Sean, I was pretty much the only on-site resident of the manor who ate them. I nibbled at it, keeping a wary eye on the wolf. He poked his head out of the tent twice to glance at me, before making his way back in to dig through more food.

He was there so long and chewing things open that the sound almost became relaxing. I dozed a bit where I sat, half a moon cake in my mitten-covered hand. Should I have been more conflicted? Run perhaps? Survival class said running was a good idea only in some instances. Stillness or not showing fear better in others.

Sometimes even getting big, screaming, and waving arms around could frighten something off. I couldn't really recall a direct face-to-face with a wolf and which scenario that warranted. But I didn't feel like I needed to run. The wolf was hungry. Maybe he'd go away on his own when he was full. There was plenty of food in that tent to fill him up. I hoped there would be enough left for Rio.

I was startled to find the moon cake pulled out of my hand. The wolf was right there. The fact that it hadn't taken my hand off to get the cake had to be a miracle. It swallowed and slurped, licking its lips as the moon cake vanished. I stared, then slowly reached back for my pack and the remaining stash of cakes. It didn't move. No lunging or any of the thousand other terrifying ideas that went through my head. I took out the container of cakes and opened it, beginning by tossing the first cake to the wolf. It caught it, barely did more than swallow it whole. Eventually I fed it the cakes, one by one until they were gone. It got closer and closer, until it sat beside me, using me as a sort of stopping point, and curling up near my legs.

Maybe it just looked like a wolf. Wolves weren't normally so tame, right? Maybe Rio had fed it regularly, which meant it had probably had a few days of being absolutely starving. I dug through my pack for more food options. I had a handful of protein bars and granola bars. Things that I normally didn't eat because they were full of junk, but I unwrapped them and fed them to the wolf. All while it stared at me with those eerie eyes. Eyes like Rio's, I realized. So clear and blue, like pools of icy frozen water. It was odd, yet I still didn't feel uneasy.

The wolf settled down stretching out its paws toward the fire, pressed to my side. I hoped it had enough food. But I carefully reached over to touch his head. He didn't move. No snapping, biting, or snarling. He just glanced my way, a questioning sort of look like I'd seen on one of Brand's huskies. I slowly began to pet him, running my mitten slowly over his head and scratching his ears a bit.

Rio must have taken care of this animal. Maybe that's why his blankets had been covered in hair, and yet he hadn't really claimed to own a dog. Who owned a wolf? I was mystified really. In what sort of dream world did I, a tiny little queen with a love for cooking, end up sitting in the dark cold after a blizzard petting a wolf?

"It's a bit like a fantasy novel," I whispered, a bit afraid the sound of my voice would startle the wolf. But he didn't move. "Maybe this is the beginning of some quest to save the world?"

The wolf seemed to snort.

"Yeah, I'm not really the save the world type, right? But I make a mean sticky bun."

He whined a little.

"I think you ate them all," I said. "I can make more, but I have to go home to do that."

He didn't move as I continued to pet him. The fire was dying a bit, chill easing into my bones and making me shiver. The wolf stood suddenly and I almost leapt out of my skin, as he turned and took a hold of my sleeve with the tips of his jaw. He tugged instead of biting. He tugged me toward the wood pile.

"Yeah, I'm on it. Fire is good." I added another log and poked at the fire a little until it blazed again. That was better. The wolf sat down beside me, acting as a bit of a break even while the wind picked up again and I shivered. "A windbreak would be nice." I glanced at the tent and wondered if I could lie down and take a nap. I was so tired. "But I'm not sure if that's safe? What if you eat me while I sleep?"

The wolf seemed to huff and half drape itself across my lap, instilling a pulsing bit of warmth. Was it his fur that made him so warm? I sighed and leaned into him. "Thanks. Don't eat me, okay? I promise I'll make you more sticky buns." I closed my eyes, thinking I really needed to stay awake, but that I was so tired I simply wanted to rest them for a bit.

CHAPTER 17

Another snarl woke me. I only jolted a little, startled awake, surprised I'd fallen asleep, and feeling a bit numb, even while my entire left side was blazing warm, and the right side of me felt like I'd been stuck in a freezer. Something was moving in the dark, then paused. I could see a vague outline in the dying light of the fire. Was it Rio? I had a few seconds of hope. The wolf growled again, but it wasn't Rio who shined a flashlight over us.

It was Zach. And behind him Sean. My heart flipped over in sadness and disappointment. The wolf growled beside me. I reached out to pet his head. Zach's mouth opened as if to protest, but the wolf calmed under my touch.

"Are you trying to freeze to death?" Zach asked quietly.

"Um, fire…" I pointed at the dying blaze. What time was it? I frowned and pulled out my phone. It was after midnight and no sign of Rio.

"Okay, caveman. Wanna tell your friend it's time to go so we can take you home to get warm?"

"Rio didn't come," I said sadly, gripping the wolf's fur a bit. "This guy ate most of the food I brought. What happens if Rio comes later?"

Zach seemed to hesitate, looking at Sean and back to me and the wolf who didn't seem interested in moving from its spot. Which was fine because he was deliciously warm.

"Montana, that *is* Rio."

That was ridiculous. "Um, it's a wolf…" I looked back at him, noting the light gray fur and those clear blue eyes. Okay, the eyes did look like Rio, but this wasn't a fairytale. "People don't turn into wolves. Because, science," I said, too tired to think of all the real reasons why.

"Not unless they are cursed," Sean said.

I slogged through a mash of confused thoughts, none of which really made sense. Rio a wolf? Rio cursed was a thing, or at least that was what everyone told me. But cursed to be a wolf? Not possible. I stared at him. He stared back at me. "Are you Rio?"

He didn't answer, just turned his gaze from me to Zach and Sean. At least he was no longer growling.

"He's not raving," Zach said, I think more to Sean than me. "Seems calm enough."

"Fed?" Sean replied.

"And if we try to take Montana with us?"

"I don't know," Sean said apologetically.

Zach stared at the wolf. "Rio. We need to get Montana home. He has to get warm or he'll get sick. You want Montana safe, right?"

The wolf turned his head and laid it across my lap seeming to let out a long sigh like he was annoyed. I ran my mitten covered hands across his head and side. His stomach seemed to rumble and both Zach and Sean jumped a little, but the wolf didn't move from his spot.

"He might have eaten all the food I brought," I said and dug through my pack, finding a single granola bar. I leaned over and kissed the top of his head. "He reminds me of my friend Brand's huskies. Less chatty though. Those dogs ramble and talk like crazy."

"He's not a dog," Zach said but sighed. "You really need to get warm."

I groaned and stretched looking around in the dark. "Can we leave this stuff for Rio? I'm not sure how much food is left, but the tent and the stove and stuff would be helpful."

Zach seemed to want to say something else but finally nodded. "Sure." His gaze fell to the wolf again.

I got up, patting my wolf friend on the head and gathered up my bag. "You be safe out here," I told him. "Take care of Rio? I'll bring more food."

The wolf stared at me, but didn't try to stop me as I threw snow on the fire until it sizzled out and then headed toward Zach and Sean. Neither of them got closer. They headed down the path toward the cars but kept looking back. The wolf was following us. I reached for him, and he came to my hands like he'd been trained to do it.

"Do you see that? He's tame," I said. "Probably by Rio. I bet he was starving out here. Maybe that was why Rio was determined to leave the manor?" If we brought the wolf home maybe Rio would come home too? "He was worried about his friend."

Zach said nothing. We found our way back to the cars. Zach had already hooked my car up to be towed by his. He rounded the truck to the driver's side, opened the door and leaned in to start it, blasting the heat. Sean opened the passenger side and pushed the front seat forward so I could crawl into the narrow back. I was surprised when the wolf moved ahead of me, leaping into the narrow space and fitting himself into the back seat, leaving only a tiny amount of space for me. I climbed up next to him, strapping on my seat belt as Sean returned his seat to normal and climbed in.

Zach stared at him, still standing outside the driver's side in the open doorway. "Is this safe?"

126

Sean shrugged. "He's fed. Seems attached to Montana. Only aggressive if we threaten him."

"Is he in there? Thinking? Seeing us? Recognizing Montana?"

"I don't know," Sean said again. "We will have to ask him." He glanced up as though he could see the sky from his spot in the truck. "Perhaps when full moon is over?"

Zach got in the truck. "Will he not change back until after the moon?"

"Sunrise," Sean said. "Human in day, wolf at night."

I felt like they were speaking a foreign language. But the wolf rested his head in my lap and the blasting heat began to really thaw me out. I sighed in relief, not realizing how cold I'd been. "I'm so not meant for winter survival training," I mumbled.

Zach glanced back at me and then the wolf before closing his door, pulling on his seat belt, and navigating us back toward the road. He said nothing else, but kept glancing in the rearview mirror the entire ride home.

He didn't park in the garage. I knew he had to release my car from the tow strap, but I was too tired to do more than stumble out. The wolf pressed to my side, keeping me upright.

"I will get them food," Sean offered, and waved his hand toward my loft area, "And upstairs."

"Is that safe?" Zach asked again, looking worried.

"Important to feed him," Sean said staring at the wolf.

"He's not going to eat me," I said. "Even wolves in the wild aren't likely to eat a person unless they are starving and find that person wounded. Science," I said again, trying to recall all the nature documentaries I'd watched in my life. Sometimes I played videos on my tablet while cooking long meals.

"How much food do you have at your place?" Zach asked.

"Restocked when we went grocery shopping. Fridge is full. Lots of crackers and stuff in the pantry. I was prepared for Rio to stay," I said. I thought about the wolf. "Meat in the freezer. I don't have fresh deer or rabbit. It's not really a grocery store staple…"

"Okay," Zach said, but still seemed hesitant staring at the wolf. "Don't hurt him," Zach told the wolf. "I'm not a hunter, but I know several. There's one surefire way to break your curse..." That sounded like a threat, but the wolf didn't react.

Sean headed toward the door to the upstairs apartments. I followed, the wolf sticking close to me. Once I got to the door and opened it, Sean hesitated again staring at the wolf. Finally he turned and reached out to trace a symbol on my forehead. It felt a bit like those church baptisms they showed in movies. I didn't feel any different when he was done. "Ward will last until morning. Small barrier in case he attacks."

"He won't," I promised, though had no idea how I would keep him from doing anything. He was bigger than me. Probably outweighed me. Was that normal for a wolf? I'd have to look it up. Maybe he was only part wolf, and mixed with some large breed dog. I sighed and went into my apartment. "I'll see you guys in the morning."

Sean seemed to want to say something else, but instead he shook his head and closed the door. I heard his footsteps moving away. I stripped out of my gear, leaving it on the rug by the door before making my way to the bathroom. I turned the water on hot, my skin cold and brain exhausted. I stared in the mirror for a minute, searching for signs of frostbite. Everything seemed okay. The wolf came in the bathroom and stared at me for a minute. When I stepped into the shower, letting out a heavenly sigh at the heat rolling over me, he laid down on the rug beside the shower.

He seemed to keep an eye on me, and I was too tired to worry much since he was acting like a dog. When I got out of the shower, feeling warmer, I tugged on a pair of underwear, dug out a pair of warm jammies, put them on, and made my way to the bed. I'd never made it that morning. Didn't a lot of mornings. Too excited to get to the start of the day and cooking. Right then it was a blessing because I didn't have to unmake the bed to slide under the blankets and nestle down.

The wolf jumped up on the bed, his weight making it move a little. I popped an eye open to stare at it through the dark. "Sleep, okay?" I asked it. "I'm cold and need some sleep. I'll make some more sticky buns tomorrow."

He settled down, draping himself half across me, which I would have protested if his fiery heat didn't suck me down into much needed sleep.

CHAPTER 18

I awoke feeling deliciously warm and well rested. The light through the window indicated either my alarm hadn't turned on, or I had somehow slept through it. And oddly enough, as my body and senses began to slowly awaken, I realized I was wrapped in someone's arms. He was wrapped around me from behind, spooning me, his arms hugging my middle, hair falling half over my neck where his face nestled. My heart did a little rolling turn from sheer joy. Rio had come back.

I let out a long, contented sigh and ran a hand down his arm in a caress, the fuzz of his hair calming. He was as warm as usual, didn't look any thinner from the little I could see nestled up to him, and I hoped he was okay. I could have stayed there for hours. Then I remembered the wolf and wondered if I would have to let it out to go to the bathroom? I hoped it hadn't peed in the apartment. I didn't smell anything, but the thought made me sit up and look around the room.

Rio grumbled, rolling back a little to let me go and rubbing his eyes.

The wolf was nowhere to be seen. Had Rio let him out

already? I hope he wasn't lost out in the snow again. How did one care for a wild wolf anyway? Even if it was half tamed?

"Where did your friend go?" I asked Rio, then grabbed my phone from the bedside table. The alarm was off. There were a handful of texts from Zach I must have missed this morning. First seeming a bit frantic, wondering if I was okay, then telling me to get some rest. Weird.

I sent Zach back a message that I was just now getting up and asking if he'd seen the wolf. Zach must have let Rio in, since I hadn't shared my key, but I wasn't sure Zach had the key either as I'd gotten it from Mr. Yamamoto who was still on break.

"Friend?" Rio asked sleepily.

"The wolf?" I prodded, staring down at him. He looked a bit scruffy and sinfully delicious. I wondered if I could keep him in bed today.

Rio stared up at me in silence for a minute. Those beautiful eyes of his wide and confused. Had the wolf not been his pet?

"Tamest wolf I've ever met if he isn't yours," I added, thinking maybe he was hiding having a wild friend.

"Only around you," Rio muttered. He pushed himself up. He was completely naked beneath the blankets. I sighed sweetly as I looked over him. And only then did I realize his bags, and the other things that contained his clothes were absent. And I couldn't see anything lying on the floor or the bathroom that indicated he'd stripped before getting in bed with me. Had he been running around out there in his birthday suit?

I stared at him. Mind slowly awakening and nothing adding up. Or at least not adding up to anything that made sense. "Rio?"

"Do you want me to go?" He asked.

"Why would you ask that?"

He picked at the comforter, gathering up a wad of hair which had obviously been from the wolf. He picked at it, and my brain went back to Zach's words last night, that Rio was the wolf. That wasn't possible. Yet things were adding up.

"Um…" I stared at him, confusion probably a big question mark on my face. "No wolf friend?" It had been real, the hair proved that…

"I am the wolf," Rio said quietly.

Those words flittered around me, an echo of thought and pulling out memories of our time together. Werewolves weren't real. It couldn't be… "Werewolves aren't real," I whispered, like I could make it true just by saying it.

"I don't exactly call myself a werewolf. It's a curse, not a romance novel trope."

I blinked at him, trying to make sense of a million things that didn't fit together, yet did.

Rio climbed out of bed. "I should go."

"You're naked," I pointed out dumbly.

"Yeah, that happens when I shift back." He glanced at the window.

"Shift… How? Why? Can you help me understand?" I was so lost for a minute, thinking maybe this was some fairytale dream, and yet staring at him and finding so many things falling into place. "Rio?"

"I have to shift on the full moon. Most of the time I spend the entire three or four days of the moon cycle as the wolf. It's easier on my brain to let it take over… eat…"

I could feel my eyes widen. Did that mean he ate people? That's what they did in the movies.

"Animals," Rio added. "Deer most of the time. And three days of feeding on raw deer is pretty gross to deal with as a human…"

"I have a dozen great venison recipes," I said without really thinking. "Not raw of course…" I floundered, not really sure what was happening. "You turn into a wolf? Because someone cursed you?" I clarified.

"Yes," Rio agreed. "Happened while I served. It was why I was released early. They'd have kept me, tried to create another unit of *special* soldiers, only they couldn't keep us fed enough." He flinched as though the memory hurt.

"But I've been feeding you."

"Promised me more sticky buns," he whispered.

I gaped at him. I had promised the wolf more sticky buns. Was this all for real? Legit? "Can you change whenever you want?"

"Yes, and no," Rio said looking away. "Changing makes the hunger worse. If I'm already hungry to start with it can be dangerous. Hard to decipher humans from prey and food. It's why I stay so far away from people. You shouldn't have gone to the trailer last night. I could have hurt you."

Instead, he'd decimated the food supply I'd brought and kept me warm. I climbed out of bed to stand near him, looking him over for signs of anything different. Did it hurt? Was it one of those scary transitions like in movies? Was I sane for even believing him? I reached out to touch his face but he backed away.

"I don't want to hurt you," he said.

"But you haven't. Are you hungry?"

He looked at the kitchen. "Was up earlier and ate. I'm okay for a bit. I need to eat more closer to the moon. The pull to shift and hunt is stronger if I don't eat enough."

No wonder everyone told me to keep him fed. I stepped in close and reached up to cup his face. He still looked like Rio. A little scruffier, but not gaunt or ill looking like he'd been when I'd first dragged him home. He did look tired, not in a lack of sleep way, but in a world-weary way.

"So, if I keep you fed, you're not a danger to anyone then, right?" I said rationally.

"If you'd asked me that last month, I'd have said no... the hunger is intense, a gnawing of need that grows until it seems to take over."

"But now?" I'd been feeding him like crazy. That had to mean something.

"I'm not sure anyone is safe, but maybe you are. The wolf seems to recognize you."

I thought about that. "You are the wolf."

"Yes," he agreed.

"But is the wolf you?"

He shrugged. "When I'm not starving? A little."

"Does the change hurt? I'm sorry. I have so many questions and I'm still not even sure this isn't some weird, undercooked hot dog dream."

He blinked at me, but didn't pull away. "I will answer as much as I can. I'm not sure the change hurts or not. I sort of black out when it happens. Both ways. Sometimes I remember bits of being the wolf, sort of like snapshots."

"You remember stuff from last night?"

"Yes," he agreed. "Not at first. Woke up this morning hungry and in your bed. Thought the worst. Only you were fine." He looked toward the kitchen. "Ate a lot of your food, then Zach showed up at the door, angry and worried. I started to remember bits of last night."

"Zach knows," I said, suddenly aware of all the things he and Sean had been saying that made no sense.

"Sean has some power," Rio said. "He kind of glows with it. He can tell what I am. Perhaps has met someone like me before."

And somehow that made sense. Why not? Werewolves were real, and my boss's lover was some kind of witch? Was there a Chinese mythology for witches? It was far too much for nine in the morning. I needed coffee.

"Let me get coffee. Is there any food left?"

His cheeks turned pink. "Very little."

I waved a hand at him as I headed to the kitchen to see what I could find. "I need coffee, and there's more food at the main house."

"I don't have any clothes. Left them out there with the sled…"

I glanced back his way taking him in again, so happy he looked healthy. "I'll send a text to Zach. You can borrow something of his and maybe find the sled?" I narrowed my eyes at him. "Because you'll be staying, of course."

"I shouldn't…" he began.

"You left because you were worried your wolf would hurt me?" I confirmed.

"Yes," he agreed.

"Worry over. I'm fine. A little stunned, but fine. We keep you fed and all is good. Maybe we can try to find a way to break the curse?"

"Only way to break the curse is with a bullet through my brain."

"Does it have to be silver?" I wondered out loud even while not wanting to think it.

"That's where your brain goes? No, any bullet will do."

"Then best you stay close where I can feed you and keep some triggered gun-toting asshole from setting his sights on you," I said matter-of-fact. In the kitchen I found he'd pretty much emptied my fridge, though I had plenty of canned options left. I threw together a taco chicken casserole, popping it in the oven. "I need to get ready for the day, get over to make lunch. But this should be done in twenty so you can snack, okay?"

He let out a long sigh.

"You're not a burden," I said before he could say it. "I don't want you to go."

"Even knowing I'm a wolf, cursed with this insanity?"

"Can I catch it?" I wondered.

"It's not an STD. I'd have to nearly kill you to give it to you."

"That would be unpleasant. It's not a virus or anything like that?"

"No. It's a blood curse. Some magic crap combined with blood."

Not that I understood that at all. But wasn't sure I needed to. I crossed the room to touch him again, enjoying his warmth and the fact he didn't run away this time. "Are there more like you?"

"I don't know. A few probably."

"No big packs like real wolves?"

"None that I have found. The rare occasion that I've met another it's been a territorial war between us almost instantly. More like the curse wants to destroy itself so pits us against one another rather than working together like real wolves."

That was sad. No wonder he was alone out here. "It happened while you were serving?"

"Our troop got in the middle of a war between two wolves. Had no idea at first. Stumbled across them. Half a dozen died. Three of us eventually changed. I'm the only one still here."

I didn't press him on that as it seemed to really hurt. Ten years he'd been out here alone, battling this curse by himself, abandoned by everyone, and left in the most vulnerable position for anyone, food insecure. I couldn't imagine being cursed with an insatiable need for food and having little access to it. But having him here at the manor, where I could keep him fed and happy, that made my heart sing.

"Do you like being here?" I asked. I waved a hand. "Even if we just fed you? You are not required to stick around me. I know I can be a bit much…"

"I can't remember a time I've been more at ease with someone," Rio said softly. "Even if there are people moving around the house and I'm hungry, all I have to do is look at you and I'm calm, the wolf relaxes a little."

"Maybe because he knows I'll feed you?"

"That's probably part of it for him. But you also see me. You don't treat me like I'm gum stuck to your shoe. You teach me things without even trying, offered kindness first, and have a passion for taking care of people." He let out a long sigh. "Waking up to you is like being alive again for the first time in over a decade. I shouldn't get attached. It's not fair to you. I'm not safe."

"But you are," I disagreed. "You haven't hurt me."

"Because you fed the beast."

"I fed you. And will continue to feed you. I'm sort of crazy about you," I said. "So, stick around. Let's work on us, yeah?"

He sucked in air. "Yeah?"

"Yeah."

I let him go and headed to the dresser to find clothes for the day. I had food to make, including sticky buns. When I turned back, Rio was still there, standing in the same spot as though frozen.

"Rio?" I asked.

"No one cared before," he whispered. "It was always too much."

"What about your family?" I asked.

He shook his head, gaze focused on me.

"Well fuck them," I said. I knew all about family abandonment. "We make our own family. And here at the manor we have a nice one. Zach never said you had to go, right?"

"No. He wants me to stay. But wants you safe too."

"I am safe."

We stared a moment longer, both of us stopped, me wondering what else to do for him to show him he was wanted here, not a burden, even with his curse. I said, "You know the manor used to be cursed? Zach broke it when he fell in love with Sean. Maybe your curse has an out clause like that."

"And if it doesn't?"

I shrugged. "Your curse just means you need to eat." I pointed to myself. "I am a chef who loves to feed people. Can't think of a better match myself. I mean, so you get a little hairy sometimes. I'm finding I'm not all that turned off by hair."

EPILOGUE

Rio spent the day in the kitchen with me. Zach had retrieved his clothes and asked him to stay close to the manor, even if he changed. I wanted to see the change, but Rio had been very hesitant. My focus was on feeding him.

Zach checked in occasionally but didn't seem all that worried. I stopped him once while Rio was helping with the firewood again, which apparently was a never-ending job in the winter when everyone loved to sit by the fireplace.

"You knew he was a werewolf?" I asked Zach.

"He's not a werewolf," Zach amended. "He's cursed."

I thought about that for a minute. "Does that mean there are werewolves too? And then people cursed like Rio?"

Zach shrugged. "There are a lot of things in this world that I didn't used to believe in. Once your eyes are open to it, it's a bit like tearing off a Band-Aid. Sometimes it's amazing and other times it's scary. Careful what you pull back."

I had to think about that again for a while. "Was there really a curse on the manor that you broke by falling in love with Sean?"

"Sort of. It's a bit more complicated, and yet a lot simpler than that. But yes, there was a curse and it is now broken," Zach said.

RECIPE FOR A CURSE

"And no way to break Rio's curse? Would Sean know?"

"No. Already asked. Most of his knowledge of Rio's curse was supplemental. Something he heard from somewhere, never really experienced."

"But if I keep him fed, he'll be okay?"

"Sounds like it."

That was good news at least. "Do you want to give me a pay cut to help pay for all the food he'll need?" I asked, thinking I could manage since I didn't have to pay for shelter as that was included.

Zach looked appalled. "No. Rio will work here at the manor with a regular salary. You'll feed him just like we feed everyone living here. In the spring, after the snow thaws, he can decide if he wants to repair or replace his trailer. For now, he'll stay here."

That lightened my heart. "He can stay with me."

"If that's what he wants," Zach agreed.

"He worries he'll hurt me."

"We were worried too. But his wolf seems attached to you."

I really liked that idea. Rio protecting me, as a wolf or human. It felt sort of archaic, but made me happy at the same time. "I guess it's a good trade-off. I feed him and he protects me?"

"Leave it to you to fall in love with a werewolf," Zach grumbled. "Like this is some romance novel and you're the swooning damsel."

"You said he wasn't a werewolf," I teased. I put my hand to my forehead, "Well, I declare. Bless your heart."

He laughed. "Brat. Close enough. Go cook. You have a wolf to feed."

"You just want more sticky buns," I said unable to keep the grin off my face.

"Yes. And damn you for getting me hooked on those. I do not need the sugar," Zach growled as he headed back to his chores.

"Tell Sean to help you work it off," I called as I made my way back into the kitchen, at home in my space with a huge need to cook. At least I had people to feed. Not much else could make me that happy. Having people to feed and Rio, who paused each time he passed through the kitchen to give me a hug or kiss my cheek, or even nuzzle my hair. It was a bit like he was marking me, but I thought of it as him finding peace in my presence and took to feeding him snacks each time he popped in.

It wasn't until after dark, when the final meal had long been put away, that Rio had insisted on going outside alone.

He asked me to wait. To give him an hour before stepping outside to look for him. And I had. Bundling up and finally finding my way to the back door of the garage with a pan full of fresh, hot sticky buns.

I heard the howl first. Close and a bit chilling as it made goosebumps rise on my arms. When he appeared, it was at the edge of the woods in the distance, moving carefully and slowly, as though not to be seen. But I popped up a small crate and put the buns on top, taking a few steps back to give him space. In the darkness he slunk toward me, dangerous and exciting all at once. Yet I didn't fear for my safety. He was too hesitant for that.

Instead, he found his way to the pan and began to slurp out the sticky buns, seeming to make happy noises as he ate. My heart swelled when he finished and licked his lips. He made his way to my side, sitting down and pressing into me like he needed me to hold him up. No aggression, though he did award me with a wolfish grin.

"This is real," I said, still incredulous. "I'm dating a werewolf." It wasn't at all like I imagined a romance novel would be, lots less fangs and claws and more slobber and dog hair. But that was okay. I could see us with a future together, and that's all that really mattered.

Read where it all began with Zach and Sean here: Heir to a Curse.

LETTER FROM LISSA

Dear Reader,

Thank you so much for reading *Recipe for a Curse!* If you enjoyed this book check out the first book set in this world, Heir to a Curse.

Be sure to join my Facebook group for fun daily polls, writing snippets, and updates on new releases to this series and others.

For a sneak peek at my work before it's published join my Patreon group. Patrons receive three new chapters a week, and many other perks. Also check out my website at LissaKasey.com for new information, visiting authors, and novel shorts.

If you enjoyed the book, please take a moment to leave a review! Reviews not only help readers determine if a book is for them, but also help a book show up in searches.

Thank you so much for being a reader!

Lissa

ABOUT THE AUTHOR

Lissa Kasey is more than just romance. She specializes in in-depth characters, detailed world building, and twisting plots to keep you clinging to the page. All stories have a side of romance, emotionally messed up protagonists and feature LGBTQA spectrum characters facing real world problems no matter how fictional the story.

Also, if you like Lissa Kasey's writing, check out her other works:

Simply Crafty Paranormal Mystery Series:

Stalked by Shadows

Marked by Shadows

Kitsune Chronicles:

Witchblood

WitchBond

Survivors Find Love:

Painting with Fire

An Arresting Ride

Range of Emotion

Hidden Gem Series:

Hidden Gem (Hidden Gem 1)

Cardinal Sins (Hidden Gem 2)

Candy Land (Hidden Gem 3)

Benny's Carnival (Hidden Gem 3.5)

Haven Investigations Series:

Model Citizen (Haven Investigations 1)

Model Bodyguard (Haven Investigations 2)

Model Investigator (Haven Investigations 3)

Model Exposure (Haven Investigations 4)

Inheritance Series:

Inheritance (Dominion 1)

Reclamation (Dominion 2)

Conviction (Dominion 3)

Ascendance (Dominion 4)

Absolution (Dominion 5)

Evolution Series:

Evolution: Genesis

Boy Next Door Series:

On the Right Track (1)

Unicorns and Rainbow Sprinkles (2)

Made in the USA
Middletown, DE
05 August 2021